CHESS FEVER

Chess Fever

Published by The Conrad Press in the United Kingdom 2019

Tel: +44(0)1227 472 874
www.theconradpress.com
info@theconradpress.com

ISBN 978-1-911546-75-7

Copyright © Mark Ozanne, 2019

The moral right of Mark Ozanne to be identified as author of this work has been asserted in accordance with the Copyright, Designs and Patents Act 1988.

All rights reserved.

Typesetting and Cover Design by: Charlotte Mouncey, www.bookstyle.co.uk
Cover image credits: Young man sitting - Photo by Gage Walker; Woman in sunflower field - Photo (model @marissa.mowry) by Blake Cheek both on Unsplash.com; detail from *Bulletin of the 29th Chess Olympiad at Novi Sad*, Yugoslavia 1990.

The Conrad Press logo was designed by Maria Priestley.

Printed and bound in Great Britain by Clays Ltd, Elcograf S.p.A.

CHESS FEVER

MARK OZANNE

For my father

Is it not also a science and an art, hovering between those categories as Muhammad's coffin hovered between heaven and earth, a unique link between pairs of opposites: ancient yet eternally new; mechanical in structure, yet made effective only by the imagination; limited to a geometrically fixed space, yet with unlimited combinations; constantly developing, yet sterile; thought that leads nowhere; mathematics calculating nothing; art without works of art; architecture without substance – but nonetheless shown to be more durable in its entity and existence than all books and works of art; the only game that belongs to all nations and all eras, although no one knows what god brought it down to earth to vanquish boredom, sharpen the senses and stretch the mind.

Stefan Zweig, *Chess Story* (1942)

Each life is a game of chess that went to hell on the seventh move, and now the flukey play is cramped and slow, a dream of constraint and cross-purpose, with each move forced, all pieces pinned and skewered and zugzwanged... But here and there we see these figures who appear to run on the true lines, and they are terrible examples.

Martin Amis, *Money* (1984)

1

My clock is ticking when I arrive at the board, eyes half-open, tongue sandpapered, throat throbbing, brain trying to push out of my skull.

The relentless ticking of chess time. Every minute more is one minute less.

Twenty minutes late – not too bad considering my morning.

The chair opposite me is empty but my opponent has left a white pawn glaring at me from the centre of the board. He's also left a sickly grey cardigan or coat on the back of the chair and a white plastic bag on the floor, jammed with what look like chess magazines and bulletins.

The run from the bus stop to the Sports Hall has winded me, and I need to take a few steady breaths, one, two, three, hoping my headache doesn't get any worse. God knows how much I drank last night, with that crazy Yugoslav.

It's good to sit down. I start to take off my black leather jacket but it's going to be difficult without elbowing one of my neighbours in the face – to my left, on Board 2, is a young guy with inch-thick glasses; to my right, on Board 4, is some guy with long hair and a scraggly beard who's staring up at the high ceiling. He looks like Animal from *The Muppets*.

I stand up again and hang my jacket, damp and smelling of ashtray, on the back of my chair. My identity badge, attached to its thick orange ribbon, ends up hanging down my back and I flap around to retrieve it, tasting a whiff of the sickly Lynx I sprayed on this morning. My right arm is aching – I must have slept on it last night. The position on Board 2 has the clean lines of a Ruy Lopez; while Board 4 looks chaotic – somehow a black knight has already landed next to white's king. I hope for Animal's sake he knows what he's doing.

No time to look at that now though – I sit down again and frisk my pockets for my Parker ballpoint. I feel the squidgy rubber of Lauren's rook keyring but no pen. Tell me I've not forgotten it. Finally, I feel its reassuring cold metal, deep in the bottom of the inside pocket, and pull it out with a confetti of fluff, tobacco flakes and a scrap of cigarette packet with *Kolia, Novi Sad – 650022* written on it. That was the guy from last night. Kolia. Proud Serb. Prouder Yugoslav.

With unsteady hand I fill in the pink-lined scoresheet – clean like the first page of a new exercise book (soon to be violated by my scrawls, crossings out and sweaty anxieties):

Novi Sad Chess Olympiad (Sahovsa Olimpijada) – OPEN
White (Bell) – F P Mitrovic (Yugoslavia)
Black (Crni) – S M Renshawe (England)
Round (Kolo) – 14
Board (Tabla) – 3
Date (Datum) – 3 December 1990

I roll a wavy line under Move Forty – Time Control. Two hours for forty moves and another hour added for each extra twenty moves. No adjournments today for the last round. We just keep playing. Which is why we're all here early in the morning and I'm feeling like death.

Not sure where my opponent is – maybe it's that bald guy down there by Board 1, although I think that's one of the assistant arbiters. Or perhaps a spectator... probably lost because spectators aren't interested in this tournament – they're all in the main hall next door watching the Olympiad. Watching the three Yugoslav teams, the Soviets, the Polgar sisters, England.

My pieces are lined up in front me, gleaming with newness, full of potential, waiting for my attention. I adjust them – *j'adoube* them – Bobby Robson tapping his players before they charge onto the pitch. Both hands work inwards from the rooks, and it's good to feel their features in my fingers – the wide girth of the rooks, the knights' slender necks, the bishops' downcast mouths, the queen's knobbly coronet, and the king's sharp cross, pressing its sharpness into the top of my finger. I do the same hand movement four times with the squat bald pawns. My queen's rook is still off-centre, and I delicately slide it across with the rigid forefinger of my right hand.

OK, they're ready, I'm ready. It's time to get to work. Time for the adventure to begin. Time to do this – a win here will give me a chunky prize and the best result of my life: second place in an international open. I wipe my clammy hands on my jeans, glance at that white skinhead in the middle of the board and flex out the fingers of my right hand. Here we go...

I lift my king's knight high over the rank of black pawns and settle him in front. I depress the cool metal knob on my clock, and the faint metronomic ticking transfers to his side.

And here he is, my opponent, the antagonist, the enemy, appearing from nowhere like Mephistopheles, filling up his seat. Short and squat with a puffy face, black receding hair, seventies side-burns, black stubble. He's wearing a creased, overlarge white shirt, top button open to black hair, battered cigarette packet poking out of the chest pocket. Chunky arms. More like a provincial butcher than a Yugoslav International Master. Wonder where he comes from in Yugoslavia. Is he from here, Novi Sad? Or has he travelled up from Belgrade or Sarajevo or somewhere else?

The Yugoslav grunts one word – was that 'hello' or something in Serbo-Croatian? We go for a glancing handshake, my fingers brushing his palm – two dead fish knocking against each other. He looks at my knight, glances at me with dark eyes in chubby sockets, and pushes another skinhead into the centre.

The physical presence of the enemy inches away from me, so close that I can smell the cigarette smoke on his clothes, the enemy who wants to strangle me, in the same way that I want to strangle him, delivers that reassuring gut-jab of adrenalin. It is with him I must struggle all day till he or I lie dead.

To my left, the German kid, in a fur-rimmed coat, is bent over the board, thick glasses nearly touching the pieces. On my right, Animal is still praying to God, his opponent's black knight poleaxing his kingside.

I check the clock faces…

Chess time: White – 1 minute
Black – 25 minutes

… and push a black pawn up to g6.

The Yugoslav lifts out his queen's knight, holding its top delicately between two forked fingers. But I've been here before… I feel a ghostly glow in my stomach as I realise that this same opponent in this same tournament hall played this same move using those same two fingers against me sometime in the past. But when was that? And what happened?

But's it's gone. I can't recapture the memory. It was a lifetime ago. It's not there...

And that's the thing with déjà vu – you only experience it once and you can't replay it because you don't see it, you feel it.

Tricks of the mind that aren't helping my hangover.

I slide my bishop into his little watchtower on g7 – hello my sad friend, good to see you rushing out there to keep us safe. Don't worry, your time will come.

The Yugoslav moves up his king's pawn and there are now three white fascists terrifying the public in the middle of the board. Another punch of adrenalin as I look at them lined up smartly in the centre – it's going to be a King's Indian Defence. Which means that later I will be launching a righteous counter-attack that will detonate those fascists all over the Yugoslav's pudgy face.

King's Indian Defence – light of my life, my soul, my sin. Not a chess opening but a way of life. King's Indian Defence. Those three words describe all that is most noble in chess: the sacrifice of everything considered valuable – space, structure, material – in exchange for an Arthurian attack on the white king. Triumph after persecution and suffering. They describe imperishable works of art conceived by Fischer and Kasparov.

It was Fischer who first peddled me the intoxications of the King's Indian, up in my box bedroom in Dartford. His *My 60 Memorable Games* was my thirteenth birthday present – postal ordered from the shop in Sutton Coldfield with a cheque written by my dad. *Are you sure that's what you want, son?* At the time, all I knew about Fischer came from the old science teacher Mr Bell, aka Zippy, at the school chess club: he was the American who had taken on the Soviets at the height of the Cold War and won.

Some books have the power to rearrange your consciousness, while the true masterpieces change your life. I didn't understand all his variations (or his Americanisms – 'pinkie', 'kibitzer', 'haymaker'), but the book exerted its power over me. It changed the way I looked at chess, but it also changed me as a person: I was no longer someone whose hobby was chess, but a *chess player*.

My bedroom became Fischer's room in his mother's shabby Brooklyn flat. The school books were cleared off my desk and replaced permanently by my chess set and Fischer's book. Homework was done on the bus in the morning, if at all – I couldn't spend time on trigonometry tables and French verbs when I had a book full of magical adventures and terrible beauty. My seat on the settee next to my mum in the glow of the weekend quiz shows remained empty while I was upstairs inhaling Fischer's variations and prose. When friends came to the door, Matthew Farmer with his pet football, I'd shuffle down to tell them I had homework to do, and burrow back into my room to be with Bobby. Before long they stopped coming. I didn't care – I was tasting the first joy of loneliness, and I was with someone who understood me, who was teaching me about chess and life – 'Sam, it's not good enough to be a good player, you've also got to play well.'

And I need to play well this morning to beat this Yugoslav. We rapidly tango down the main line of the King's Indian Defence. The steps we take, followed thousands of times by thousands of dancers throughout the decades, conveying their messages. The Yugoslav's are saying, 'Yes, my friend, you can play like this but I am going to take all the space, and give you a bad bishop, and squash you all over the board à la Petrosian,' while mine are saying, 'that may be so, but I'll have enough space to kick-start my pieces and my bishop will not be bad for ever, and I'm going to counterattack like Kasparov. You can enjoy your space while your king is sitting in a pool of blood with his guts hanging out.'

We exchange the odd pub glance, trying to glean more information. Who is he? What motivates him? What does he *do*? He's fairly low-rated for a professional player. Is he a guy who never made it but can subsist on a handful of dinars for teaching kids in the Yugoslav equivalent of the Pioneer Palaces? Does he have a family to support back wherever he lives, or is he alone with his chess board and magazines?

I suppress, with difficulty, a belch. I must have had one of those giant burgers last night after I left crazy Kolia in that pub. And what was that poisonous liqueur he was plying me with before I left? A memory of the sweet bleachy liquid going down my throat shakes me with a frisson of nausea. I can't remember what it was called but it's split my head open and dehydrated me and I need to go and get a coffee… but my opponent retreats his king's knight to d2 for his ninth move, skewering me back in my chair. He looks at me from under his heavy black eyebrows as if asking, 'And what do you think of that?'

The first thing I think is that young knight on d2 has dangerous ambitions to stomp into my queenside behind a storm of white pawns. That's why Fischer preferred now to play a blocking pawn move on the queenside to slow up the white avalanche. That's what he did when he destroyed Korchnoi somewhere in Yugoslavia, not Novi Sad, twenty years ago on his way to winning the World Blitz Tournament by about six clear points. That is the game in which, the battle raging, Fischer sent his developed knight back to h8. When I first saw the artistry of Fischer's concept – re-energising the knight in that forgotten corner square before leaping it back up the board to smash against white's kingside – it gave me such a high that I had to leave my bedroom to calm down, as if I'd overdosed on too much beauty. I went downstairs with my pocket set and grabbed my dad, drowsing in front of the gas fire and the snooker, to show him what I'd seen. Maybe I didn't explain it very well, but it made me sad when I realised he neither appreciated nor understood it.

The second thing I think is that you know I always play Fischer's move. I most recently played it in the British Championships in Eastbourne back in the summer. That game – a grisly loss – was not published anywhere but could you somehow have seen the tournament bulletins?

But what you don't know is that I've spent many hours recently working on an alternative to Fischer's pawn block – the immediate knight retreat to d7. With this move I spend no time slowing up White's attack on the queenside – I let it come – and push on with my assault against Black's king. The 'Get-On-With-It' variation. It looks mental and no one plays this direct approach anymore because white's invasion on the queenside comes quicker than Saddam Hussein's tanks screaming into Kuwait. It's the King's Indian at its rawest – you stake your whole queenside for a chance against the white king – your life support machine is flat-lining and before they turn it off you have one against-the-odds chance of resuscitation. There is nothing else after that. Just the way I like it. But it took me many hours, and the discovery of a fantastical rook sacrifice, to convince myself that Black can stay alive long enough to have that one chance.

You don't know all this. You also don't know that seeing that knight sitting on d2 lashes me with a painful memory of Lauren – walking in and surprising me in the bedroom, then two doors slamming as she left my flat for the last time. But I'm not going to start thinking about all that now.

It's time to play 9...Nd7 for the first time in my career. Until now it's just been a dream on my pocket set. Sorry Bobby, I don't usually ignore your chess advice but trust me on this one. I scrawl down my move and cover it with my Parker. I flex out the muscles on my right hand. Here we go…

2

The Yugoslav looks at that knight on d7, looks at the free run he's going to have on the queenside, and wipes a meat-cutter hand over the back of his mouth, as if in anticipation of the butchery he'll soon be enjoying. There is nothing for him to think about – all restraints are off – he grabs his panting b-pawn and hurls him up the board.

I take the smooth bald head of my f-pawn between my thumb and three fingers, and move him in a smooth parabola (giving the little fellow a bird's eye view of the battlefield) to f5 where I ensure he is in the dead centre of the square. First contact with the white fascist centre. It doesn't matter how many hundreds of King's Indians I've fought in the last decade, launching that f-pawn always gives me a pulse of excitement, a rush of battle commenced, of the bugle sounded to let slip the hounds.

I was a wide-eyed teenager when Fischer first showed me the idea of retreating that king's knight to allow the f-pawn to advance and then putting the knight back, as if the pawn has magically moved through the knight. I liked it so much that I was performing the trick in every game I had the chance, without realising that it only works when the centre is closed.

Fischer didn't tell me that – I guess for him it was too obvious to mention.

But here the centre is locked up like a fist. The board resembles two regions divided by a mountainous border, and civil war has ended all movement and communication between the two. I'm only making moves on the kingside (sailing my guys towards his king's fortress), he's only making moves on the queenside (commandos already charging up the beach), as if we were playing on two separate boards. The moves play themselves (and are still book) which is good for me because I need to clear my head before I do any thinking.

But on his eighteenth move, the Yugoslav leans his forearms on the table (cheap silver digital watch with no functions on his hairy right wrist), and seems to consider things for the first time.

The minute hand on his clock is still almost vertical, mine is pointing straight down:

Chess time: White – 2 minutes
Black – 30 minutes

Jesus, what have I been thinking about?

And what could the Yugoslav be thinking about in this position? Does he know about the Bath Variation here? Or is he considering it for the first time, as I did back in the summer during the football World Cup when I discovered it, preparing for the British Championships in Eastboure? The seemingly deadly sacrifice of his knight on d6 that destroys my position and looks winning for White.

I had not left the flat for three days, spending the day on the tatty settee going through variations while the football matches played silently on the TV in the background, striving to bring the 'Get-On-With-It' variation – 9... Nd7 – back to life. And I was nearly there when Lauren floated into the flat wearing a long floral summer dress, sleeveless, displaying her slender brown arms. She didn't comment on my pyjamas but pulled apart the heavy velour curtains, opened the window, removed the empty coffee cups, Kit-Kat wrappers, and Cherry Coke cans from the dusty coffee table (she left the copies of *New in Chess*, *Inside Chess*, *British Chess Magazine* and *Chess*), and switched off Des Lynam's suave, moustachioed face. It took me a few moments to adjust to the censorious sunlight, the uninvited breeze, and Lauren's presence.

'It's so lovely outside, and there's no riots going on today, so we're going out for a walk, and you're not bringing *that*.' 'That' was my plastic pocket chess set, sitting guiltily on the arm of the couch.

'OK, but I might need to have a bath first.'

'Yes, I think you might.'

While she went into the adjoining kitchenette to make herself a tea, I padded to the tiny bathroom, my set weighing down the pocket of my cinnamon dressing gown. Submerged in the soap-scented womb of the warm water, chess set floating on the surface, I checked again my latest variations. I was feeling confident that I had resurrected 9... Nd7, and let the set float away from me. I was hoping to play it over the board against a strong player in the upcoming British Championships. I tipped my head back under the water, imagining a shell-shocked grandmaster, hair awry, glasses skew-whiff, barely able to sign his score sheet after I'd battered him with a scintillating king's-side attack... forcibly reminding commentators of Piket-Kasparov,

Wijk aan Zee, 1989. 28... Nh1. Double exclamation mark. What a finish!!

When I came back up for air I opened my eyes and looked at my pocket set bobbing against the tap-end, and saw for the first time that White could sacrifice his knight on d6 on move 18. I lunged for the set, nearly sinking it, and studied the position. But it didn't matter what I tried with Black, White was smashing through in all variations – the sacrifice was winning. Which meant that 9... Nd7 was unplayable, simply losing – a discovery to be sure (maybe an article in *Chess*), but not the one I was looking for. But surely someone had already found this? I needed to check my books (Geller, Keene and Botterill, Markovic, MCO, Martin), but how to do this with an already pissed-off Lauren lurking in my flat?

I steadied the floating set on the water and started moving the little guys around...

A drumming on the bathroom door. 'What the hell are you doing in there?'

I turned to the door, sinking the pocket set like a torpedoed battleship, some of its crew freeing themselves and going down separately. 'Er, I think I must have nodded off... I'm getting out now... sorry.'

'Well, hurry up, will you? I want to get out in the sun.'

There is an antidote to the Bath Variation, rather an obvious one (although it wasn't obvious to me). In fact, the knight sacrifice loses for White, but I didn't find that out until long after Lauren had left me, one door slamming after the other.

It should have been refreshing to be out in the warmth of the sunlight but my mind remained in the dark flat, working on the chess position. We took the tube to Putney Bridge and as we walked to the Heath, Lauren was telling me about her plans to visit Germany as part of her research in the next academic year, but it was hard to concentrate on what she was saying because that white knight kept thumping down on d6. Crossing the bridge, under the implacable blue sky, the river underneath was so low that there were wide stretches of dank sand that reminded me of the beach at Margate.

It was so hot that it was a relief to enter the sappy tree smells and partially shaded lanes of the Heath. As we walked on the paths, patchworked with light and dark, my brain was working out variations stemming from the knight sacrifice. But I couldn't remember where one of the black pawns was – the diagram had become hazy in my head – I badly needed the clarity of my pocket set.

'Sam – do you think you'd be able to do that for me?'

'Sorry, do what?' I think that pawn was on a6 rather than a7.

Lauren suddenly stopped in an oil spill of shade. She looked at me, a fleck of sweat on her small nose. 'Sam, are you listening to anything I'm saying?'

'Yes, of course I am – sorry, I was just thinking about that stupid-looking dog we passed.' So, if the pawn were on a6, that variation wouldn't be viable.

She frowned. 'What stupid-looking dog?'

'Er, back there, when we came onto the Heath, there was this dog that looked like a monkey.' But I just can't remember where that pawn should be, which would change everything – I need to get away from here, out of the trees and heat and shade, and clarify everything on my pocket set.

She glared at me. 'Sam, what're you talking about? Are you there? What is wrong with you? I'm telling you loads of important stuff about my plans for next year and whether you could come to Germany with me, and do some of your PHD there, and you're talking to me about dogs and monkeys. Are you remotely interested in anything I'm telling you?'

I need to wash these variations out of my head. 'Yes, of course, sorry, Lauren. You know, I've got loads on my mind at the moment, thinking about where my thesis is going and stuff.'

'Look, Sam, I think we need to talk.'

'OK, well, that sounds ominous. What's wrong?'

A runner came pounding down the track. Crew cut, tight England football shorts, blue singlet, headphones attached to one of those flat portable CD players which he was holding in his hand. How does the CD not jump around while he's running? We moved out of his way and sat on a bench.

'We need to talk, Sam.'

'Yeah, so you said... what about?'

Lauren leaned her head back slightly, looking up into the tree canopy. 'What about? What about? Come on Sam, things haven't been right for a long time now.'

'Not been right?'

'Yes, not been right. Between you and me. I just can't ignore it any longer. This isn't something sudden, something today. Things haven't been right between us for a long time now.'

'You think so?'

'Yes, I do think so. Sometimes you're just not there.' She shook her head. 'Sometimes, I just don't know where you go.'

A dark-feathered bird – a crow? – hopped onto a knee-high wooden post near the bench. I wondered what the post was for… it looked like a giant black pawn. On a6 or on a7? But I needed to concentrate on Lauren. I looked at her squinting eyes. 'You know, I've been concentrating on my PHD.'

'No Sam, you've *not* been concentrating on your PHD. That is exactly what you've *not* been doing. You've been spending all your time playing chess. Well, not *playing* chess exactly, not against another human being, just playing against yourself. Sitting in your flat playing against yourself.'

I tried a small laugh. 'Well, you know, I'm not really playing against myself, as such. You know, I'm reading magazines and books and studying some of the theory. You know, I've qualified for the British Championships for the first time, and it's important to me, and I've got to do some preparation for it.'

'Yes, so you keep telling me. But all day? With the curtains closed? To the exclusion of your university stuff? To the exclusion of your friends, our friends? To the exclusion of me? I'm sorry Sam, but I mean we just don't seem to do anything together anymore.'

'Well, we're out now, aren't we?'

'Yes, we are, we are out now, but we wouldn't be if I hadn't come into your flat and literally dragged you out of your pyjamas.'

She sighed. She looked at me. 'Look, I want the Sam back who takes me to places, to see things, who wants to *do* things… together. We haven't been out in ages, even to the pub, or the cinema, or any exhibitions, or…'

'We went to that Shakespeare thing at the National Gallery last month.'

'Yes, we did, but only because it had stuff about an Elizabethan chess player.'

'A Victorian chess player – Howard Staunton. But come on, that was just a small part of it.'

She sighed. 'Elizabethan, Victorian, Postmodern chess player, I don't care. I don't want to argue about it, Sam. That was over a month ago and it was something you wanted to do.'

The crew-cutted runner bounced back through the clearing, breathing audibly, sweat dribbling down his face. That sweat must have soaked the orange sponge of his headphones. A variation from the knight sacrifice came chopping back into my head – pawn takes, pawn takes, knight takes, bishop drops back, and white queen comes in… but I can push the queen out. Anyway, I can look at that later. Refocus on Lauren.

Lauren also watched the runner before she said, 'I want the Sam back who wants to do things, who reads to me in bed, who makes me laugh…'

'Look, Lauren, I'm really sorry, you know how I get with things sometimes – I get wrapped up in my bubble. It was like with that thing I was trying to write at Christmas, you remember that?'

'Yes, I remember,' she said, leaning her head back again, looking up at the fragments of pristine blue between the trees, her fair hair hanging behind the back of the bench. 'But you weren't like you are now. I've not heard from you for nearly a week. What've you been doing?'

'Yeah, sorry, I've been doing a lot of studying…'

'No, not studying, don't call it studying, Sam. Reading books on chess, you mean. Have you even started writing any of your PHD yet?'

'I've done a lot of thinking about it.'

'For a year? You've been thinking about it for a year. You

weren't like this when I met you. You didn't even play chess then. You always told me that you used to play when you were a kid but had given it up. Why did you start playing again this year?' There was a whiney undertone to her voice.

Because I was getting bored with my life. By the life that everyone else seemed to enjoy. University research, university girlfriend, university friends, pub quizzes, walks in the park… *hot water at ten and a closed car at four.*

'I don't know… I just wanted to have another go at it. Just to see if I could get anywhere with it. And now I've qualified for the British Championships.'

'But does that mean you have to spend every minute on it? Does that mean that you have to ignore everyone else completely?' She exhaled a puff of air up into her fringe. 'Look, Sam, do you actually want to be with me?'

'Hey, Lauren.' I placed my hand over hers. 'Of course I do.' I did want to be with her. And I didn't want to be with her. Queen takes, pawn up, queen retreats somewhere… Where? a5? Doesn't matter.

'Because I'm just not sure that you do anymore.'

'No, I do, I really do, it's just, I don't know, it's just that sometimes…' Sometimes, all I wanted to do is think about chess. Sometimes, I just wanted to be left alone so that I could analyse important opening discoveries. Sometimes, playing through a cut-glass positional squeeze by Karpov was more interesting than listening to her. Sometimes, I needed to go to a tournament so that I could take all I'd learnt and experienced and felt about chess and crush the ego of another player who was trying to do the same to me.

She removed her hand from mine. 'It's just what?'

'I don't know… it's just that sometimes I can get a bit insular, a bit wrapped up in what I'm doing.'

'Yes, so you keep saying.'

'But yes, I'm sorry, that's not fair on you, and I don't want it to be like this, I'm sorry – I want to make you happy, I really do.' I took her hand again.

'Well, you do. You do make me happy. Some of the time.' She smiled for the first time. Lovely Lauren. Did I really want my lovely Lauren to slip away?

'But you know Lauren, you're right, we haven't been anywhere for a long time. I know what we should do tomorrow, let's go back to Margate. Take the train down for the day. It's always good there on a Sunday.'

'Margate?'

'Yeah, why not? You loved it last year, didn't you? We'll have a laugh. And I'll treat you to Dreamland again.'

She managed another smile. 'And you won't bring any of your chess books or magazines, or anything to do with chess?'

'No, I promise – I'll even leave my rook keyring behind.'

'Look Sam, I'm serious.'

'Yes, so am I, and I'll bring nothing – except my swim suit.' And maybe my pocket set hidden in the back pocket of my rucksack.

'OK, then. I'll have to check that they won't need me on Sunday evening, but it could be nice.'

And I'd have to cancel my entry in the Islington one-day tournament.

We took the tube back, surfacing on Euston Road as the yoke of the sun broke onto the tops of the buildings. The silvery top of the Telecom Tower looked like one of those rooks from an oriental set.

Lauren wanted to make dinner – 'You're not eating Super Noodles tonight' – and we stopped off at Sainsbury's to buy the ingredients for a shepherd's pie. I looked longingly at the rows of dewy black and white Carling Black Labels in the fridge but I didn't have any money, and Lauren pulled out a cheap bottle of rosé wine to 'celebrate the summer'.

I needed to adjust to Lauren's brightness inside the cave of my flat, her blonde hair and floral dress contrasting with the dull interior; the smell of her citrusy perfume and coconutty sun cream emphasising the lingering coffee and lager mustiness. I was mentally prepared to spend the evening with her – no chess, no football (USSR against Costa Rica) – but I couldn't stop thinking about that white knight sacrifice. I needed to look at it on my pocket set. If only for a few minutes. Just a quick look to answer some of the questions I'd had on the Heath.

She was preparing the meal in the kitchenette – cleaning, peeling, chopping – 'Do you even own a knife that's sharp enough to cut anything? And can you get the table ready?' By which she meant clear away all the copies of *New in Chess*, *Inside Chess*, *Chess* and *British Chess Magazine* strewn over the coffee table.

'Yeah, give me a minute. I'm feeling a bit knackered to be honest. From all that sun. I can feel a headache coming on. You don't mind if I have a quick lie down while you're doing that?'

Small blunt knife in one hand, she looked at me. 'Well, OK. But this isn't going to take very long. Have you taken any aspirin?'

'Yeah, I'll grab a couple now. And thanks.' I leant over the knife to kiss her on the lips. 'Thanks, for all this, for everything.'

I took a glass of water and two aspirins from the kitchen into the bedroom and softly clicked the door. I needed to be quick. I retrieved my pocket set from the saggy pocket of my dressing gown hanging on the rail. I replaced it with the two aspirins. The set was still damp after its earlier bath, but it looked ready for action – hello again, my old friend.

I stripped down to my underpants and slipped under the duvet, sitting back against the headboard. I drew up my knees, making a ski-run of the snowy duvet, and rested the set on my stomach.

Rapidly setting the position up, I flexed my right hand and stuck the white knight into the watery hole on d6. It was satisfying to have my hands touching the pieces again – the blind man with his Braille.

I didn't have long, but I had to see how bad this was for black. So, let's go from the beginning. You've got to take that knight of course, no other option. OK, so that pawn is still on a7 – does that change things? Of course it does. Queen takes pawn, pawn up, queen retreats – so now she can go to a5. And if she can sit on a5 what can I do here? Wait, I've got knight there, that could be good for me. No, that's nonsense, that's nothing for me. Zilchville. He's taking all my pawns. God, this is just winning for White, I just don't know what Black can do to defend. But let's be systematic about this, I can still play bishop takes…

'What are you doing, Sam?'

I tried to pull the sheet up to hide my crime, but in my panic, I upended the set and it leapt off the bed onto the lino.

Most of the pieces jumped out and skittered across the floor.

'Are you playing chess?' She was staring at me viciously, eyes shining. 'After all we've been speaking about? While I'm in there cooking dinner for you?'

'Yeah, sorry, I was feeling a bit better – those aspirins worked well – and I just thought I'd have a quick look at something…'

'That's it, Sam.' She looked down at the tiny dead figures strewn across the floor as if brought in by the tide, at a Lilliputian white knight near her black DM. 'I can't do this anymore. I can't do this.'

She did an about turn and slammed the bedroom door, echoed seconds later by the thunderclap of the flat door.

Two days later, I received a letter:

I can't do this anymore, Sam.
I still love you to bits but you're just not making me
happy anymore.
I never wanted to be your 'past tense' but I see no other way,

Lauren

3

Anyway, enough of all that. That's all over. You're here now. This is what you want to be doing: playing chess. This is where you want to be: the Novi Sad Olympiad Open punting for second place. This is who you are. Time to focus on the here and now. Time to beat up a Yugoslav.

And does the Yugoslav, sucking his pen opposite me, know that the Bath Variation loses for White? And if he doesn't could he tempt himself into the unsound sacrifice of his knight? A quick win for me and second place in the tournament. Surely God wouldn't be that kind? But maybe it would be some sort of cosmic justice for all the pain that the Bath Variation caused me. But you can't beat a Yugoslav master that easily. I'm sure he knows about it even if it's not in the books.

And even if he is looking at the sacrifice for the first time, any decent player should be able to find Black's refutation in a couple of minutes – it was only dunderhead here who took a hundred hours to find it. The obscure we see eventually. The completely obvious takes longer.

The Yugoslav leans further forward, breathing in the pieces, and I'm sure he's looking at my d6 pawn – but what sequences are flashing through his brain? Could he really be about to throw his knight off the parapet?

I'm breathing more rapidly, heart drumming against my ribcage – hope he doesn't notice. I need to relax. I hold my breath, but he's going to notice that as well. I should get out of the way and go to the drinks stand, but that will alert him to something as well – I might as well tap his shoulder on the way out and say, 'Hey, my friend, sacrificing your knight on d6 looks like a haymaker but don't do it because Black has a crafty move which wins – trust me, I should know because it cost me my summer and relationship to find out.'

Instead, I look at Board 2. The German kid is opposite that little elderly Yugoslav guy Andic who beat me in Round Four – my worst loss for a long time, the sort of nightmare that lingers for days afterwards and you don't want to think about because it was disgusting and shameful. Andic is as dapper as he was when he played me – beige suit with a red pocket square, grey crew cut, trimmed grey goatee, precise and efficient in his movements, more like a surgeon than a chess player. After our game I was too sick to analyse much with him and he was more interested in talking about politics, in his plodding but good English, telling me about Yugoslavia's regions and about 'Big efforts by the Croatia region to ruin the country,' and asking me about Britain, why Margaret Thatcher had resigned and who would take over. I told him I didn't know and that I needed some fresh air, anything to get away from his clinical stare that had tortured me over two adjournment sessions.

Board Four is a street brawl and Animal seems to be taking all of the punches, that black knight still sitting in the guts of his king's position. His opponent, another Yugoslav, looks like the Tooth-Fairy from Michael Mann's film, *Manhunter*. The serial killer. Same big bald head and rubbery downturned thick lips, same psychopathic stare, directed at poor Animal.

High along the far wall, just below the grey PVC tiled ceiling, is a series of windows through which I can see the sheet-metal morning sky. Those high windows look like the ones in my favourite room in the University Main Library back in London. Tournament halls always remind me of libraries: that same guarded hush, high-voltage concentration, stooping figures shutting out the world in their quest to discover the truth, to deaden the drumming of the demon in their ears.

I sense the Yugoslav glance at me. I look back down and his pincher-like fingers are scuttling above the board.

To his far left – my close right, near my aching forearm – he juts forward his a-pawn, deeper into the creaking carapace of my queenside.

4

And I suppose it was never going to happen, he was never going to sacrifice that knight. That would've been too easy for me. But did he consider it? Did he analyse it and then find the refutation? As I did – although only after many hours, not two minutes like it should have taken, causing me to hurl my pocket set against the bedroom door. Or did he already know about this unsound sacrifice – mentioned somewhere in a Soviet book or magazine. I should've learnt Russian and subscribed to *Shakhmatny Bulletin* like Fischer. You know, I still could… big advantage to a chess player to be able to read Russian – maybe I'll see if there are any Russian courses at the university when I get back to England…

Or maybe it didn't even cross his mind, and he was thinking about other things – about previous games in this line; about how he'd like a sweet hot coffee; how the coffee can wait until his pawns have torn apart my queenside like the vultures on Prometheus' chest (if they learn Greek mythology in Eastern Europe); or how many dinars he'll win when he beats up this pale, clueless, crazy English guy.

If I don't drink a coffee soon I'm going to pass out.

I'll have to ask him after the game what he was thinking

about, although even then I'll never really know. You never do see all the thousands of thoughts that cannon around a player's brain during his five hours of chess time. Every chess game leaves a scoresheet with forty or so moves, which we tap through on our set, but we never see all the thoughts and human emotions lying behind them – the hopes, the drug-like excitement, the rushes of creativity, the suicidal lows.

It was in Frank Brady's biography (which I went on to read about twenty times) that I first saw a photo of one of Fischer's scoresheets – his masterpiece against Donald Byrne. I ogled it for a long time, trying to glimpse the essence of his written moves, the genius behind his '11_NR5' and '17_BK3', but to my disappointment they gave me nothing. Like music scores and poetry manuscripts, scoresheets are just records, neutral carriers of huge passions and creativity. I felt the same when I first saw Shakespeare's handwriting in a manuscript of *Sir Thomas More* at that exhibition in the National Gallery. I wanted something that just wasn't there.

Not that anyone will ever be able to read my own scoresheet. We're only on move eighteen and it looks like I've written the moves on a ship in a storm, standing on my head. Or like the scribblings of a political prisoner whose mind is fragmenting under the pressure, like that guy in Stefan Zweig's novella *Chess Story*. What was his name? Did he even have a name? Can't remember, but I need to start recording my moves sanely.

OK, so we're still in book here. Following a game from the mid-eighties between two Soviets – Someoneovitch against Vykhovsky in Batumi, referenced in one of my *Chess Informator*s to show why you don't play the 9... Nd7 line – Black gets snuffed out before he's even had a chance to knock on the door of White's king's position. I take about thirty seconds to write down my move, the schoolboy concentrating on his handwriting, and then advance one of my knights on the kingside, another of Vykhovsky's moves.

What was Vykhovsky's opponent called? Rabinovitch? Zitovich? Zlivovitch? *Slivovitz* – Jesus, that was the paint stripper we were drinking last night, and the word unlocks another memory of the sweet liquid going down my throat, accompanied by a fresh shiver of nausea.

My opponent instantly makes another no-nonsense knight move on the queenside, and I'm convinced he knows the Batumi game. He is merrily following the Batumi game. But does he think I don't know it and am ignorantly following Vykhovsky off the cliff, or does he think I do know it but have managed to cook something up. Which I have…

And it looks like I'll be able to unleash that discovery which changes the assessment of this variation – the Patrick Moore Sacrifice. Vykhovsky, seeing that his a8 rook was about to exit the board stage right, started making defensive moves on the queenside. The rook survived but only to look on guiltily as all around him burned, his kingside troops still in their barracks as White's stormtroopers piled in. Soon Vykhovsky was shuffling out of the tournament hall with his towel for an early swim in the Black Sea.

Once I'd recovered from my beatings at the British Chess Championships and the break-up with Lauren, I started trying to find a better way for Black. One night I returned to my flat from the Green Man and was feeling good about things, partly from the four pints of Carling Black Label I'd drunk, partly because of Kasparov's win against Karpov in

New York the day before – I could still hear the crunch of 25. Bxh6 – but mainly because I'd logged the high score on the pub's pinball machine.

I sprawled on the settee with a fridge-cooled can of Carling, a microwave-heated chicken pilaff, my pocket set, and the beige-covered *Informator* from 1984, idly looking at the Batumi game again, seeing if Vykhovsky could have avoided his early bath, the television buzzing in the background – Patrick Moore's Churchillian face presenting *The Sky at Night*.

After another Carling, I put the set down and imagined presenting a late-night TV show called 'Chess at Night', highbrow and intellectual, during which I'd conceptualise for viewers the three elements that constitute the chess universe – space, material and time. I'd use the Vykhovsky game as an example: Black has no *space* on the queenside or the centre, but he does have some on the kingside; *material* is equal; but Black is way down on *time*. He needs about four moves on the kingside. How to get more time? Only by exchanging it for one of the other elements, only by redistributing the elements which make up the one chess *hypostasis* (slurp of lager). Black can't give any more *space* to get *time* – he doesn't have any left – so he must give from his *material* element. He must give *material* for *time*. In life, we do the opposite – give up our time in exchange for money. However, some do it the other way around, preferring to take the time rather than the material, such as poets and artists (slurp). In the Vykhovsky game black needs to be that artist… he must give up that beach-front villa on the queenside in exchange for some free time to paint his masterpiece on the kingside (burp). He must sacrifice that rook…

To the cosmic music at the end of *The Sky at Night*, I dunked down my lager can, hoiked up my pocket set, and started to move the little guys around, trying to see if Black could really give up a whole rook, five big points, in exchange for a couple of tempi on the kingside. I brewed up some potent attacks against the white king; I mixed some mouth-watering checkmates. I created one sinuous variation culminating in a queen sacrifice, that was so beautiful I needed to write it down. I heaved myself up to find a notebook and realised that the Test Card was keening loudly, the little girl and her clown haunting my living room. I staggered to the set and switched it off, and forgot why I'd left the settee, so I careered into the kitchen to fetch my last two cans of Carling. My lovely pocket set was patiently waiting for me, and I dived back into the position, discovering another trove of magical variations, surfacing only to inhale Carling. When the morning light started peeking in through the curtains, trying to see what was going on, I was tired but satisfied (and completely pissed). I tottered into my bedroom falling face-first, fully-clothed, onto my duvet, convinced that the whole thing from 9. Nd2 was a forced win for Black (even Kasparov didn't know this), and, my right cheek nestling on the cool pillow, I fell asleep grinning stupidly at how I was one of God's chosen ones when it came to pinball and chess.

Towards mid-morning I awoke with a headache, a deep thirst and a dry sense of unease.

I made a mug of strong coffee and a tower of toast, smeared with peanut butter. I ate it on the beery settee, feeding my wall-eyed hangover, while reading the latest blurry Ceefax report on the Kasparov-Karpov match – Karpov was taking a time-out to recover from the bruises that Kasparov's Bxh6 had given him. My pocket set was lying on the coffee table with its own hangover, its pieces strewn about lifelessly – a white knight had drowned in a puddle of lager.

I wanted to look at the rook sacrifice again but in the reality of the cold autumn sunlight I was afraid of what I might see.

After preparing myself with four aspirin, washed down with another strong coffee, and the lunchtime showing of *Neighbours*, I cleaned up my pocket set and gingerly started to move the pieces around. I couldn't rediscover all the chimerical lines of the previous night – that fairy-like queen sacrifice had dissolved into the mists – but I did find some solid possibilities for Black. In front of the afternoon coverage of the Conservative Conference in Bournemouth, fortifying myself with Cherry Coke, I methodically wrote down my research. By the time my hangover had cleared, as *Red Dwarf* was starting, I had half-filled a notebook with variations. Some of it was no doubt nonsense, but before donning my leather jacket to go to the Green Man, I felt confident enough to draw a thick ➔ after the kingside pawn move that initiated the rook sacrifice – 'with attack'.

And now, as I carefully write down that move – '21... h4' – I must resist the urge to add that 'with attack' symbol on the scoresheet; my favourite *Informator* symbol, pointing to the potential for imaginative brilliance. There is nothing in chess that compares to the pure pleasure of assailing the enemy king. You can stop worrying about everything else – weak squares, cramp, bad structure, lost queenside rooks, dry throats and headaches – and use your creativity to lead a charge that has one goal only: sticking the dagger deep into the enemy's windpipe.

I carefully lay my pen over the secret that I will soon reveal to my opponent and the world, the move that Vykhovsy and everyone else failed to see, or *saw* but did not *think* what I thought. It will set in train the loss of my queen's rook for scrap metal on the kingside that I will have to transmute into Kasparovian gold.

I take a last glance at the position in front of me – hello my old friend, your time has come – and a quick look at my queen's rook to convince myself that it is a worthless lump of plastic. I stretch out the fingers of my sweaty hand, and, with the buzz of a novelist on the publication day of his masterpiece, shunt forward my h-pawn. Here we go…

5

Chess time: White – 5 minutes
Black – 39 minutes

I expect my jab to cause some bodily reaction in the Yugoslav, but he continues to stare vaguely at something behind my head as if I hadn't made a move at all, let alone a move that leaves a whole rook hanging and overturns years of scholarship on this opening. But I'm sure that he has felt the blow and is trying not to show it. Without looking at the board, he knows what I have done and what it means. He slowly writes my move down and, lizard-like, turns his face to my advanced h-pawn, then to my queen's rook, back to the h-pawn, before homing in again on the rook. A free lunch.

And the overriding emotion I sense is greed. A whole rook waiting to be devoured. He has hungrily entered the factory canteen for a bowl of borscht and is surprised to see that the trestle tables are sagging under the weight of an all-you-can-eat feast. But there is also a sliver of suspicion – he has seen a stranger in the corner who looks like a secret policeman. What does he do? Help himself to the food and hope that the policeman has come for someone else? Or pull back, leave the canteen hungry... and make a defensive move on the kingside which might be more sensible and even necessary, or might make no difference at all. And the guy must make this decision in a nose-bleedingly complex position that he has never considered before.

I am pleased to see that his forearms are back on the table and that he looks like someone about to start an unpleasant but necessary piece of work, like the monthly deep clean of his butcher's shop. Even if it's not fully sound I love my Theoretical Novelty. When I get back to London I'm sending an article on it to *Chess*, demonstrating its inaugural victory in Novi Sad, explaining how I found it, and why it's called the Patrick Moore Sacrifice. 'Young Englishman demonstrates his out-of-this-world TN that stunned Yugoslav IM in Novi Sad.'

Chess time: White – 8 minutes
Black – 39 minutes

And the best part of it is that it's coffee time while he's thinking. Thank God for that. A just reward for my cleverness.

Outside the playing hall, the corridor air is cool and refreshing against my cheeks; it also smells less stale out here. I turn right towards the drinks table. To the left self-absorbed players are flowing to the smoking area. There's Keith Stetson from West London, the only other British guy in the Open tournament. He was also with me at the Lloyds Bank Masters during August. He's looking down at his clumpy 'Mr Men' shoes as he jerkily shuffles past and doesn't see me.

No more smoking at the board in FIDE tournaments. It

makes for a different atmosphere inside tournament halls. They've always been redolent of cigarette smoke, coffee and sweat – the smell of my youth. Now it's just coffee and sweat. However, at the Lloyds Bank Masters, played in that subterranean room of the Cumberland Hotel near Marble Arch, smoking was still permitted for some reason, despite the FIDE ban. It was funny when that French guy resigned against the Rumanian defector Mihai Suba and then blew up, shouting about Suba's chain smoking throughout the game, blaming it on his loss. Old Suba sat back in his chair, bemused, cigarette still blazing, smoke curling around his head, while this guy ranted at him. Actually, it was a bit distracting – I was playing a few boards away, against a Soviet female master, although I think by then I was already lost. Next to me was big James Howell, thumbs in his ears, hands visoring his eyes, who didn't notice a thing – 98% concentration compared to my 2%. In general, I wasn't concentrating well in that tournament and it was a bad one for me, although it was good to see young Micky Adams stick it to the Soviets and Eastern Europeans. It was also good to see the Hungarian Ildiko Madl and the Yugoslav Alisa Maric in London. I fell in love with the first, and in lust with the second, although I spoke to neither of them.

At the long drinks table, I take one of the plastic cups of water and drink it, and then another, rehydrating like a marathon runner, washing the dust from inside my mouth, salving my throat. I wait for an ageless player to finish filling a cup at the silver coffee drum. Then it's my turn to pull down on the black plastic tap, the same texture as a chess piece, freeing the black steaming liquid into my polystyrene cup, warming it like a bath. I add milk and sugar with a toothpick plastic spoon and head further down the corridor to the Olympiad playing hall.

Aw, that's good – hot, sweet, life-giving coffee – scorching my lips, the best drink in the world. It's not Nescafé but it tastes good. Chess and coffee. From the Fischer days up in my bedroom, with cups made by my mum, coffee has fuelled my chess investigations. The perfect cup is two teaspoons of Nescafé Gold, two teaspoons of brown sugar, mixed with one teaspoon of Coffee-mate. That was the blend that recently sustained me through my Olympiad training regime – measuring out my preparation in coffee spoons:

1st Coffee – (mid-morning) in bed to rehydrate the hangover

2nd Coffee – on the settee with my breakfast (CocoPops followed by toast and butter), reading the latest Ceefax report on the Kasparov-Karpov match

3rd Coffee – opening preparation (King's Indian)

4th Coffee – (stirred with a couple of Kit-Kat fingers) – continue opening preparation

5th Coffee – (mid-afternoon) with my lunch (a cheese and pickle sandwich packed with Wotsits)

6th Coffee – (by now the hangover had usually cleared) – tactics from *Informant's Encyclopaedia of Combinations*

7th and 8th Coffees – (around the second showing of *Neighbours*) – a Kasparov game from *Test of Time*

Cherry Coke – (to rehydrate from all the coffee) – recent games from the magazines

Carling Black Label – a few games of pinball in the Green Man to come down from the caffeine and chess high

That was the regime that resulted in the novelty that is hurting my opponent now.

At the end of the corridor a young scruffy guy – jeans and T-shirt, isn't he cold? – is guarding this back entrance to the Olympiad proper. I flash him my chess player's badge, a blanched Samuel Renshawe (ENG) with toilet-brush hair and redrimmed eyes. The guy looks bored and maybe I should entertain him with my morning story, about how I'd been waiting in the cold but clear morning for the players' bus and through the haze of my hangover realised that I didn't have my pass, and had to run back to my room in the accommodation block to grab it, only to miss the bus and join the pensioners and prams on the public one. But I don't have time (my opponent might already have moved and set my clock ticking), so I nod at him and enter the huge playing hall.

Into the pulse of the greatest chess show on earth. Ever since I'd spent a half-term holiday working through the immense Botvinnik-Fischer match from the Varna Olympiad in 1962 – 'Game 39 – The Encounter' – with its multitudes of chess and life, I'd wanted to go to an Olympiad. At that time, of course, I thought I'd be leading out England as Fischer did the USA, and not blowing the last of my university grant on coming to play in a side-event. But anyway, here I am…

And this is it – this is chess life: a football-pitch sized hall containing row upon row of chess players, male and female, representing most of the globe's different nationalities, ethnicities, political systems, and languages. The United Nations of chess. There is a low hum from the tapping of pieces, the thudding of hundreds of clocks (chess clocks – there are no real clocks anywhere), scraping of chairs, and the muffled whispers of spectators, journalists, arbiters and the black-clad student helpers, but the hundreds of players remain dumb, communicating only through the language of chess.

There's the Mauritius team in heavy coats and hats lined up against San Marino; the colourful Angolans taking on the serious Yemenis; the Vietnamese nervously battling the implacable Mongolians. Down one of the rows I see Korchnoi (Game 36), the old Leningrader, in suit and tie, on Board 1 for Switzerland giving a lesson to some Egyptian guy in a charity shop pullover. Nearby sits his tiny wife, handbag on her lap, protecting her husband like Mrs Nabokov. Wolfgang Uhlmann – Fischer's old adversary from his four Olympiads – is over there on Board 3 for East Germany against Sweden, leaning back in his chair like a senior bank manager. He's unlikely to be selected for the next Olympiad in two years when East and West are set to unite in a single team. Diagonally opposite him is Pia Cramling, playing for Sweden's men's team, her delicate features crumpled in concentration. There's Simen Agdestein, sitting up tall in his existentialist black roll neck, looking athletic even at the board – Norway's number one chess player and a striker for their national football team – an improbable combination of cerebral and physical achievement in one guy.

But I mustn't linger – I want to see how England are doing. They're at the far end of the room under the electronic demonstration boards. Coming into the last round they're in second place – they won't catch the Soviets who are way out in front, but they're almost guaranteed silver as they're one point ahead of the Americans who are playing the Bulgarians (tough mini-Soviets), while we've got Cuba – not even a team of grandmasters. I'm proud to be part of the second strongest chess-playing nation in the world. Gone are the days when the pipe-smoking, tweed-suited amateurs like Thomas, Atkins and Alexander were making up the numbers at Hastings and Margate.

It's been a great year for English chess: a match win against the Soviets at the Reykjavik Team Tournament; first place for Nunn in Wijk aan Zee; both Speelman and Short in the Candidates again; Micky Adams and Stuart Conquest ripping it up at the Lloyds Bank Masters. With Adams still only eighteen or nineteen, and a pack of other young masters hungrily joining him in the hunt, things are only going to get better. And it's been a good year for England in general: semi-finals in the football World Cup and Thatcher – poll tax tsarina and Europe cockblocker – dumped out of Number 10.

There's already a bustle of spectators around the top matches. It's a Monday, but the locals are staying away from their offices and factories this morning. Careful not to spill coffee on anyone, I jostle through the crowd to the England-Cuba match.

But what's this? The pieces on Boards 1 and 2 have been reset and the chairs are empty. Both Short and Speelman have taken quick draws. So, now it's a half-match – Nunn and Chandler both settled comfortably at Boards 3 and 4 working to bring the boys back home. But it should be OK, Nunn's opponent isn't even a grandmaster, and Chandler is breathing fire. Even if they both draw, the Americans would need to beat the Bulgarians 3.5 – 0.5 to overtake us. Almost impossible.

Although, it looks like the Americans are going to give it a go – lined up determinedly at their boards, leaning into the challenge: rug-headed Seirawan, balding Benjamin, curly-haired Federowicz, and blond De Firmian.

Suddenly, Seirawan has disappeared and I see Fischer on their Board 1 instead, and he's not aged, in an immaculate brown suit, handsome young face staring intently at the board, willing the victory with head and gut, as he did when he led the Americans out to smash the Bulgarians 3.5 – 0.5 in Leipzig, 1960. 'I give 98% of my mental energy to chess, others give 2%.'

Yes, sorry Bobby, I know, I know, I should be getting back to my board…

But a quick look at your old enemies first – the Soviets, cruising to their gold medal against Iceland. Boris Gelfand in a drab grey blazer is hunched over Board 1, twirling a captured black piece in his right hand, staring through chunky NHS glasses at a point slightly to the side of the board, ferociously calculating variations. Gelfand is on Board 1 instead of Ivanchuk who's taking the last round off, shielding the little Icelanders from his monstrous chess. Ivanchuk, only twenty-one, younger than me, and already number three in the world. He's my tip to win the Candidates and challenge Kasparov who's going to win his match against Karpov. I played through all his games from his tournament wins in Tilburg and Manilla to see how he did it, although a lot of it was hard to grasp, a bit like reading *Finnegans Wake*. He *seems* to play under a different set of general principles to everyone else, but underpinning all the freakery there is a profound inherent logic – it's chess for the nineties. These two, Gelfand and Ivanchuk, could dominate chess this decade in the same way that Kasparov and Karpov did in the eighties.

They're the future of Soviet chess, but will there even be a Soviet Union at the next Olympiad? The Soviet Empire appears to be unravelling. Estonia, Latvia, Lithuania don't want to be part of it anymore, and they came knocking on the door here in Novi Sad. They were turned away this time, but they'll keep knocking, and will shoulder-barge it down if necessary. And they'll be joined by others. Who knows what new nation states will be in Puerto Rico in two years. It's not clear that Gorbachev will manage to give enough concessions, or use enough force as he did in Kasparov's Baku, to hold things together. His people want what we have: liberal democracy – the only political system that works. They've had enough of one-party rule, 'ideological purity', 'being a good Soviet'. The Cold War is game over. You may have won the chess, but we won the history.

And I must return to winning my own chess war. But a quick detour on the way out to have a look at the women – the top boards and the chess pin-up Alisa Maric. There's an even bigger crowd in front of the women's top boards than the men's. Around the shoulder of a denim jacket and lustrous mullet I see the three little Polgar sisters lined up against Czechoslovakia – Zsuzsa, Judit, Sofia. *Polgaria*. They all look calm, as if they're hosting the elder Czech ladies for afternoon tea, but beneath the sweet exteriors lies lethal resolve. Fischer once said that he could give any female player knight odds – well, he wouldn't be able to give any of the Polgars knight odds, that's for sure. Judit has already served up the heads of grandmasters and could even go on to beat Fischer's record for the youngest ever grandmaster. Unbelievable. Hard to understand how she's become so good at such a young age. But there's something about chess that lends itself to child prodigies. And music and maths. But not literature. Fischer was creating works of art at thirteen but there's no lasting literature written by a child…

Mullet shifts slightly and I see Ildiko Madl, the fourth member of Team *Polgaria* – they've left her out today for the final charge against the Czechs. She's standing behind Zsuzsa but looking at Judit's position. Bashfully beautiful, she is leaning forward slightly as she tries to puzzle something out on the board. She breathes upwards into her blonde fringe and the gesture fills me with a vague sadness.

I should've called Lauren after she walked out of my flat back in the summer. But I went to that tournament in Islington where everything connected, scoring four out of five, including a Kasparov-inspired winning attack in the last round that gave me such a high that I couldn't sleep on the Sunday night, replaying, reimagining, reliving all the alluring variations, and reminding me that chess was beautiful enough to waste your life on. Then, after that weekend I became absorbed in the Bath Variation – desperate to find the answer to the knight sacrifice – spending the day at the coffee table, writing out reams of notes. Telling myself that I'd call her after I'd solved it.

But I didn't solve it. And then I started my preparatory work for the British Championships in Eastbourne: setting my openings in order, solving combinations, a Kasparov game a day. Curtains drawn, images from the football World Cup silently flickering across the television screen, enjoying having the whole day to study without any distractions from Lauren.

I still thought I should call her – and that I *would* call her – but she hadn't called me and maybe some time apart was for the best. I wanted to see her, but I also didn't want to see her. I wanted to be back with her, but I also wanted to be alone. Thus, I double-thought my way through July, and, by the time I packed my rucksack – mostly chess books – to go to the British Championships we still hadn't spoken.

But they beat me up in Eastbourne. The grandmasters and masters, they eyed me up, and they knew straight away that I wasn't one of them, wasn't made from the same stuff, hadn't done my time. And they wouldn't leave me alone. They tripped me up at breakfast, they gave me a slap before bed, and they were waiting for me in the showers. They did me over in Eastbourne.

Two weeks later, badly bruised, I returned to my flat, my hired box, on a lonely Saturday afternoon. I needed to recuperate. I needed some help.

First I went to Kasparov – the 'Mr Miyagi' of Baku would show me how to deal with those British thugs. I placed a huge mug of Nescafé, a KitKat and my pocket set on the coffee table and opened *Test of Time*. But Kasparov didn't understand me, wasn't listening to my needs. He was from a different world to mine – big-money, grand stadium, high-concept matches against Korchnoi and Smyslov – all of this was no use when a ginger-haired street fighter from Gravesend comes at you with his Stanley knife. I closed *Test of Time* and made another coffee.

What about my old love, Fischer? Surely, he'd be pleased to see his former pupil and old friend. I randomly opened *My 60*

Memorable Games. Game 25. Lombardy. 'When the Maroczy didn't bind.' But Fischer's words and moves weren't binding for me. Fischer didn't want to know me – still pissed off that I'd moved away from him as I grew older.

I couldn't look at chess anymore.

I needed to talk to someone. I thought about going to the Green Man but I had no money after Eastbourne, and there was no one to talk to in there anyway – only a pinball machine I didn't want to play. I turned on the television and began to watch an episode of *The A-Team*, turning the sound off after five minutes, and the television off five minutes later. I stared at the wallpaper above the television for a long time.

I looked at the two framed photographs on the bookshelf with its missing shelf and protruding nails. My father in Margate, slitting his eyes at the camera, raging against the light. And, also in Margate, a polaroid of Lauren and me, taken by a passer-by when we visited last year, our big eyes smiling over the top of a mountainous pink cloud of candy floss. Lauren's perfectly composed blonde fringe. Lauren. I wanted her with me sitting cross-legged on the floor, rolling one of her cigarettes, looking up at me on the settee. I needed her. I needed to talk to her. She would be back home in Surrey now for the holidays. Praying that my phone wasn't disconnected, I dialled her parents' house.

'Hello, can I speak to Lauren, please?'

'No, Mrs Fairfield, it's Sam. Sam, Sam Renshawe.' Remember me? I was your daughter's boyfriend for the last year.

'OK, well, do you know when she'll be back? I'd like to talk to her if possible.'

Pause. Lauren's red-trousered father entering the hall, putting on his driving gloves?

'Oh, is she? OK, and do you know when she'll be back? From the inter-railing.'

No.

'OK, but do you already have an address for her in Berlin, somewhere that I can send her something?'

No.

'Right, OK, thanks… no worries for now, and if you do get an address… well, thanks, bye for now.'

I swallowed two aspirins with the cold dregs of my coffee. It had zilch impact, so I took another two with some tap water. I went to lie on the fusty duvet of my bed but couldn't sleep, my mind full of images of a black leather-jacketed Lauren with a heavy rucksack catching a train at a continental station.

I went back to the settee to watch some more television, four channels of shit to choose from – quiz shows, a sketch show, a police drama.

I tried to read a Shakespeare sonnet but couldn't understand it.

I took two more aspirins, choking them down dry, and went back to lie on my bed, laying my pocket set on the pillow next me. I stared at the whitewashed ceiling, unable to sleep.

I picked up the moody pocket set and started to tap the pieces around, violently, trying to animate it, jerk it into a response. I mindlessly moved into the Bath Variation – which I'd stopped looking at before the British Championships, unable to refute White's knight sacrifice.

I thumped the knight into d6 and saw a simple bishop retreat by Black that pushed White's queen away after the sacrifice. And I knew immediately that was the reason why White can't sacrifice his knight on move eighteen, why the Bath Variation is unsound. The no-frills bishop move short-circuits White's attack and leaves him a knight down. It was obvious. But like the husband suddenly realising that his oldest friend is his wife's lover, I refused to believe it. I couldn't have missed something so obvious. I started scrambling the pieces around, revisiting, reconstructing, reimagining. No, that just couldn't be. You couldn't do that to me. But I needed no more evidence, the answer was right there in front of me on the pocket set that was staring up at me insolently. The little bastard, he knew, complicit in all those wasted hours. In a murderous rage, I flung the set at the wall. It gained in height before smacking the door with a crack, and deadweight dropped to the floor, the pieces bomb-bursting out and scattering in all directions.

I lay on the bed drained of energy but unable to sleep.

I got up to inspect the damage to my set – it had suffered an ugly fracture in its side but had survived. On my hands and knees on the dusty lino I started picking up the pieces and reinserting them. One terrified white knight had skidded under the bed, and, as I peered into the semi-darkness to retrieve it, I saw Lauren's pink DMs. One was upright, and the other on its side, a piece of modern art. Her favourite pink boots. Dead. Waiting for her fragile legs and feet to walk in them, dance in them, bring them back to life.

I curled up in a foetal position on the floor, and started sobbing so violently that I had difficulty breathing. And as I did so my right cheek rubbed against the lino, leaving a red mark that was visible the next day.

I didn't look at chess again until the Lloyds Bank Masters tournament in London the following week.

Lauren. What are you doing now? Right now, at this moment, on this Monday morning while I'm staring at Ildiko Madl who is kibitzing the Polgars? I guess you're in Berlin somewhere – are you standing on the icy pavement of a street looking at a second-hand clothes shop window, in your black DMs of course, wrapped up in your oversized green army parka, with your furry purple cloche covering your blonde hair, in your big glasses, trying to puzzle out a handwritten German sign in the window? And are you leaning back slightly as you do when you're concentrating on something, rather than leaning forward like most people? Like Ildiko Mladic. And has some German student spotted you, and is he looking at your lovely face, burnished by the cold wind?

6

I clasp the refilled polystyrene cup and re-enter my playing hall, my heartbeat increasing with the return to combat. The Yugoslav is leaning back, his right arm up, orang-utan style, clasping his head with his hand, trying to *j'adoube* himself. My clock is ticking:

Chess Time: White: 28 minutes
Black: 42 minutes

So, he's only just made his move, probably while I was pouring my second coffee.

He's started his queen on her zig-zag manoeuvre towards my a8 rook. He's gone for the greedy option, but it's also the best move – get stuck into the banquet, eat as much as you can, and hope that the indigestion doesn't kill you on the kingside.

The bittersweet coffee is burning off the last wisps of fog in my head. The headache is now reduced to a pound-coin-sized throb in the left side of my skull. I'm hoping that by the time I start to do some real thinking, calculate some variations, the hangover will have dissolved completely. Not much to think about here, though. After my work on this position in the last weeks I won't need to compose my own lines for a few moves. While the rook on the queenside awaits his execution, his counterpart on the other side will lumber into position to provide long-range support for the attack. I haul my king's rook up one square.

The Yugoslav stops trying to screw his head back into his squat neck and leans forward, beefy arms back on the table, staring at my a8 rook, envisaging it off the board. But he knows that there will be a price to pay, that much is clear.

His queen's knight is slightly off its square – a millimetre or two of its base has crossed the line into the adjacent square. I'll have to adjust that when it's my move, slide it back into the centre of the square.

To my left, on Board 2, the gentlemanly build-up continues, although the mask of civility will soon drop, and the barbarism will begin. The German kid is still wearing his arctic coat, hands in its pockets, right leg pumping up and down like a pneumatic drill; Andic, bolt upright, is delicately patting the side of his mouth with his red handkerchief, as if he were between courses at a dinner party. He was doing the same thing when he tortured me in that purgatorial ending he won. Precise dainty dabs at the side of his mouth. Murderously annoying. I still can't believe I lost that. Rook and bishop against rook. Especially as I'd lost it once before in a tournament game and spent hours with Averbakh afterwards, seeing how to draw it. Andic just kept going like a machine and we came back for two morning adjournment sessions. I was playing my moves quickly, confident I had the knowledge to draw easily, happy to wander around, drinking coffee, kibitzing the other endgames. Until it went wrong, and I had to put the coffee down and start concentrating, desperately scrambling to save it, Andic calmly dabbing his mouth with his handkerchief. But it was already too late. I'd had the theoretical know-what but not the practical know-how; the knowledge, but not the wisdom.

To my right, on Board 4, White's kingside is leprous, decaying, ready to drop a limb. The Tooth-Fairy, pursing his rubbery lips, looks like he's chloroformed his next victim, while Animal stares out at nothing, fiddling with a pawn, wondering if there's a better world out there.

The Yugoslav taps his queen forward, clunks his clock and leans back in his chair, arms folded. His queen is in the inner lair of my queenside, teeth bared at my queen's rook. There's no saving him now even I wanted to. I shuffle my other rook, hale and hard-working, in front of my king. I forgot to straighten out his knight down there… next move.

The Yugoslav glances at my healthy king's rook, and it's a look of contempt, of superiority, of conviction that that rook is lightyears away from causing him any hassle. But I'm sure there is also a microfibre of unease – no chess player likes an enemy rook opposite his king, no matter how much plastic is between them.

However, his gaze soon shifts back to my queenside and, with a squint of resolve, he leans his whole body forward, almost standing up, and wraps his fat left hand around my rook, lifting it off the board, like the Cyclops pulling up one of Odysseus' men, then moves his queen into the vacated square, slowly, deliberately.

Like a grandmaster in a simultaneous display against the doddering club octogenarian in the first game to finish.

Satisfied clunk of his clock.

7

And that's it. Whatever else happens in this game I won't be using that black rook. It's now a dead lump of plastic – carefully placed behind the clock on the Yugoslav's side of the table; it's never going to chase down pawns, terrorise queens, cut off kings.

It's as if I've lost my right hand early in the battle, hacked off at the wrist. I'm looking at my devastated queenside and the kingside where my attack is yet to begin and I'm feeling that loss. All five lives of the rook. Wiped out. I want my rook back, I want it standing happily in its corner awaiting its future. I want to go back a few moves, wind back the clock and save the guy, keep him alive, protect him from the fangs of the white queen and that fat fist...

Come on Sam, that's just nonsense. Don't be one of those guys who wants to cling to his material, to use it as a measure of his success, and to mourn its loss. That's what Vykhovsky did in Batumi and look what happened to him. This is going to be OK. You've assessed it for many hours – in bed, on the settee, in the bath, on the cuckstool. That rook was of no use in its corner – it was worth zero points not five points. It's all about my attack on the other side – material is time and time is material, they're both of the same substance, and I'm merely swapping one for the other.

He's lopped off my right hand, but I'll heave up the cutlass with my left hand, and charge forward, slicing and swishing towards his king. May the force of Kasparov be with me. Keep going. I leap one of my knights closer to his king's position, followed by a reassuring sip of coffee – happy aroma, comforting press of polystyrene against my lips, warm bittersweet liquid – this is all going to be OK.

Chess Time: White: 33 minutes
Black: 47 minutes

The Yugoslav is biting his lower lip, looking more like the village idiot than the butcher. He has his booty, his full five points of rook, stashed over there in the shadow of the clock. He's done his pillaging, now he must do his defending. How to rearrange his pieces into the tight space of the kingside? And it's not easy – it was trying to put together the Rubik's Cube of White's position that convinced me the Patrick Moore Sacrifice was worth a punt. And I had my pocket set and a hundred hours in the peace of my flat, whereas he has a few minutes over the board in a pounding sweaty tournament hall.

That knight of his is still askew... annoying, must straighten that out when it's my move. I drain my coffee cup; the sugary dregs make me want another. I want to see how England are doing anyway, and another walk will be good for clearing the residual wisps of fog from my brain. I leave my opponent, chomping on his pen, frowning through calculations, like a schoolboy in a maths exam for which he hasn't revised.

Murray Chandler is leaning forward over his board, both arms gently crossing each other on the table, blond fringe hanging down above his glasses. Monk-like concentration. 98%. At one with his position, at one with chess time. Probably take him half a minute to realise where he was if you disturbed him. Next to him is John Nunn, leaning back, hands in his lap, looking out at the spectators. His black leather jacket hanging on the back of his chair looks a bit like mine; in fact, John Nunn looks a bit like me, an older smaller version, although a hundred times better at chess. It's going to be OK.

Jon Speelman, with his mop of hair, hands on hips, is looking up at the demonstration boards from hunched shoulders – evidence of all the hours he's put in bent over the chessboard. That's the thing with Speelman, he's done his time. He's feted for his endgame ability, but that's because he's put the hours in, sweating over the analysis board – like Fischer alone in his mother's flat in Brooklyn when he was a teenager. He's got his hands dirty moving the pieces around, finding out for himself the underlying mechanics of the game.

In his book *Analysing the Endgame* he asks himself one question: what is the objective assessment of Fischer's 29... Bxh2 in the first game of the 1972 World Championship match? Not why he played it (we know why) but what was it worth. And he keeps going until he has an answer. Toiling over forty pages or so to dig out the truth.

But what is chess truth? As Pontius Pilate might have asked Jesus if he'd been a chess player. I suppose it's something like an ELO rating of 5,000. That could represent perfect play – the Perfect Form of chess truth. And when we push around the pieces in the hush of our flats, that's what we're striving for, to look away from the shadows to glimpse that reality. And that's what Speelman did with the position after 29… Bxh2 – taking it to the limits of analysis and concluding that the position is a draw. Probably. We can never know for sure because of the infinite complexities of chess. Our analysis, as detailed and punishing as it is, might come close but will never achieve that perfect vision. But we can aim for it, we should aim for it – that is our goal: to come as close as humanly possible to seeing that truth.

And will computers ever get there? Will they ever be able to solve chess and show us that perfection? Not in my lifetime, that's for sure. The chess abyss is too vast, too long, too wide – it's not an earthly abyss, but a cosmic one, a black hole. I'm not even sure that computers will be able to beat the best players in the world this millennium. Deep Thought managed to beat old Larsen but was mashed up by both Kasparov and Karpov. It can crunch through a million moves or something per second but without any understanding. Chess is more than just he goes there, I go there; more than just number crunching. Even if it could look at one hundred million moves per second it wouldn't be enough – it still wouldn't make up for that ineffable human intuition that turns chess into an art. I agree with Kasparov: once a computer beats the chess world champion it will also be able to read the best books in the world. When a computer can read *Ulysses* it will be able to beat Kasparov at chess. And that's reassuring to me.

Not sure what Speelman is seeing now as he stares up at Nunn's position, although I need to get back to finding my own truth against the Yugoslav, with a quick stop for another coffee. Speelman was with me at the British Championships in heat-waved Eastbourne, although he was up on the top boards chasing Plaskett while I was getting stomped on in the cellar. God, that was a nightmare tournament for me. I was eating poisoned pawns that were always fatal, firing at the enemy king with blanks, and offering increasingly larger sacrifices that were never enough to appease the gods. It was gutting after all the problems it caused to get there.

'Shwee go?'

Lauren looked down at her almost-empty glass of cider.

'Or d'you want another?' I said, hoping she didn't. I didn't have much money and would need it for the trip to Brighton the next weekend for the British Championships Qualifier.

'No, it's OK – I've got stacks of work to do tomorrow.'

'Are you coming back to the flat?'

'Have you got some of those chicken Super Noodles?' She flashed her game show hostess smile.

'No, I think I've only got the beef ones left.'

She pouted. 'Oh, I only like the chicken ones. Come on, let's buy some chicken ones on the way to yours?'

'OK.'

'But, I should say now that I'm going to have to leave early tomorrow. I've got to go to the library in the morning to do some reading for that Research Methodology lecture.' She stubbed out her roll-up in the chunky Guinness ashtray. 'And it's going to be a busy week. We've got the pub quiz tomorrow night, and then Charlene's birthday bash on Thursday. And then we've got my parents' fete thing at the weekend. You've remembered that, haven't you? I know it's a little bit dull for you, sorry. But they do it every year and it's sort of important for them.' She drained the rest of her cider and pressed the back of her hand against her lips. 'Shall we go?'

Should I tell her now or wait until I'd made her some Super Noodles?

'Yeah, you know I wanted to talk to you about that, actually. Next weekend. You know, I'm really sorry but I don't think I'm going to be able to make your parents' thing.'

She pouts again, this time seriously. 'Why not?'

'I've got to go down to Brighton for this chess tournament.'

'You've got to go down to Brighton? What do you mean you've *got* to go to Brighton? I've already told mum and dad that we're going to give them a hand.'

'Well, I mean… you can still go… but I'm sorry I'm going to have to give it a miss. I was going to tell you earlier, but I was trying to get out of it. But it looks like I'm going to have to go.'

'What do you mean you were trying to get out of it? You choose whether you go to play chess or not, don't you?'

'Yeah, I know, of course… but I mean… I entered it a long time ago when I didn't know we would be doing anything that weekend. And now I can't cancel it. I checked with the organisers,' I lied. 'And I really should go… it's an important one. It's a British Championship qualifier, so it's really my last chance to get into the British Championships. This summer. In Eastbourne.'

She shook her head. 'Well, OK. If you must. If you must do it, if you must go, but mum and dad will be disappointed. They were banking on our help. And I'm a bit disappointed, Sam.'

'Yeah, I'm really sorry, but you can still go.' I hoped she wouldn't want to come to Brighton with me – I needed to concentrate fully on the chess there.

'Well OK, alright, if you must go, then... but you've been playing a lot of chess recently, haven't you? You missed Astrid's thing last month... and now you're missing mum and dad's fete... it's just... I don't know, when I met you, you said you didn't play anymore...'

The wail of an aggressive ambulance came in through the Green Man's entrance, the double doors pinned back to let in the sentimental spring air.

'Well, I still don't really. Not properly, I mean. Not like I did when I was a kid. But, I don't know... I don't know how it happened really... I just started thinking about it again... and then looking at it again. And now I want to give it another go. Just to see if I can get into the British Championships this year. But I'll never be as serious as I was when I was younger.'

'Well, you seem to be quite serious now.'

'You should've seen me when I was a kid. I was either playing chess or asleep.' I smiled. She didn't. 'My friends wouldn't see me for a week.' I didn't tell her I didn't have any friends. 'Look, I've got too much on now to go back to that sort of commitment – you know, with my PHD and writing and stuff. And with you, of course.' I placed my hand over hers on the wooden pub table. 'You're my addiction now.' I grinned at her.

She smiled but it looked like an effort.

'OK, you still coming back to mine for something to eat?' I said, wishing that I could be alone to look at the new *British Chess Magazine* that was waiting for me on the coffee table, glossy and clean.

'Look Sam, sorry, I'm not that hungry really, and I'm quite tired and I've got that lecture early tomorrow and... I'm thinking I should just go back tonight?'

'OK,' I said, and she went back to her student accommodation and I went back to my flat, to be alone with my pocket set, to find out how Karpov had made minced meat out of Timman in Kuala Lumpur.

8

Back in my playing hall, armed with a fresh coffee, I see that the little black button of the Yugoslav's clock remains elevated. Fantastic – no time wasted during my walkabout. He's catching me up:

Chess Time: White: 45 minutes
Black: 47 minutes

He's trying to eat his pen, his right hand supporting his flabby cheek, his left hand caressing the crenellations of the captured black rook. He doesn't seem to notice my return. I carefully insert my cup of coffee into the empty one by the clock – a pleasurable fit. I can hear the base of my new cup crunching the sugary remains in the previous cup, although I might be imagining it.

I'm feeling a lot better now, from the coffee and walks, and from seeing my preparation unfold on the board – hours of work on my pocket set in autumnal London racking up bonus points on this tournament board in wintry Novi Sad. I lean back in my seat grasping my double cup. This is what I should be doing. This is where I belong.

The full team are around me. To my left, the German kid

has his face close to his pawns as if he's going to pick one up with his mouth – bob a pawn. Opposite him, Andic is straight-backed but focused on the board, where the hooliganism is about to start, and I'm not sure which side I prefer. I'd need a few hours and coffees to work it all out.

To my right, Animal is nervously stroking his straggly beard. He's staring down at his position as if it's something embarrassing that he doesn't want to own up to – a pair of soiled underpants on the school changing room floor. And it does look bad – he's given up a pawn for the privilege of *being* attacked. He's barely out of the opening and he's almost lost – I bet he wishes he'd had a tub-thumping novelty like mine. His opponent, Pavlovic, the Tooth-Fairy, is looking around the tournament hall, searching for his next victim.

Where is his home? Where will he be going back to? Where's my opponent from? He's a Yugoslav of course but is he a Serb from around here, or a Croat from the west, or a Slovene from out near Italy – near the Trieste of James Joyce? Or he could be a Croat who lives in Belgrade, like a Welshman in London – or a Serb who lives in Zagreb, like a Londoner who lives in Cardiff? Can you tell from the names like you can in Britain? Fluellen from Wales, Gower from England. Pavlovic, Mitrovic, Andic – would a Yugoslav know where these guys are from? What was Tito? A Serb or a Croat, a Bosnian, or something else? I don't even know. But as Kolia, my drinking buddy from last night, said, it doesn't matter. *We're all Yugoslavs.*

'Hey man, unlucky, good game, good score – you play well, man. But you must hit more of little robots.'

My last ball had raced between the two flippers and dropped

out of existence. The machine's bright lights had gone out and the freaky music had stopped – game over – the bleak end to a game of pinball.

In my tunnel concentration I hadn't noticed this guy kibitzing me. He was about my age, taller than me, with a long craggy face and shoulder-length black hair – black jeans, white T-shirt, black beaten-up leather jacket. He was holding a big bottle of *pivo* in one hand and a cigarette in the other. 'You want to play again? Against me?' German accent through his gravelly smoker's voice.

'Yeah, why not? Thanks.'

'For a beer? We play for beer?' He smiled, shaking his empty *pivo* bottle.

'Yeah, why not? Although I've never played this machine before. Just getting used to it.'

Cigarette in mouth, he dropped a coin into the slot and the machine came back to life with its whirr of lights and flashes of spooky music. 'You go first, man, and I play music on jukebox.'

I prefer to play pinball on my own. A way to relax after looking at chess. Earlier that evening I'd seen the last round pairings for the following day, pinned up in the entrance hall of the accommodation block. *Mitrovic*. I'd holed up in my room going through my opponent's previous games in the tournament bulletins (there were none in the two *Informators* I'd brought). I profiled him like a detective at a murder scene in an American cop show, like the FBI guy at the start of *Manhunter*. Looking for his style, his understanding, his weaknesses. My guy was solid, he liked control, strove for clarity, didn't like being attacked. After a couple of hours assessing his chess psychology and coming up with my game plan – basically, rip his stupid head off – I went out into the ice-cold night. I found this tiny late-night place by the river – with its homely smell of beer and cigarette smoke, sticky lino floor, reliably unfriendly locals, and a pinball machine at the back between a cigarette machine and the wooden slide-door of the toilet.

Now I was getting hustled by some German guy. But I was up for it. As Pink Floyd's 'Time' ticked into action, I zoned in on the machine and controlled my ball like Gascoigne, sending it on a series of lucrative pillages up the table. Tuned into the machine, I felt like I could keep my ball going forever; I'd still be playing when they shut up the bar in the morning. I felt invincible. But that's as fatal a feeling in pinball as it is in chess, and, sure enough, like a mountaineer missing his grip, I mistimed the flip and my beautiful ball fell away for ever.

'You have played good, man. That is hard to beat.'

There are two types of pinball players: those like me who stand calmly in front of the machine as they work the flippers, and those who like to dance around following the arcs of the ball with their body. This lanky German guy was like Mick Jagger. But despite his manic energy he was always careful to avoid tilting it. And he was good. I quickly realised that he knew the machine intimately, had written the Batsford manual on it. He won a multi-ball and kept all three balls in play for about five minutes, his body swinging left and right like a juggler on a unicycle, ringing up a huge score.

When he'd finally lost all his balls, he lit up a cigarette with a satisfied look on his lined face, like someone who could eat a Fruit Pastille without chewing it. He was older than I first thought, maybe late twenties or early thirties.

'Well played.' I offered my hand. 'That was impressive. I

think you've played before.' I fake smiled. I nodded towards his empty bottle. 'And I think I owe you a drink.'

He smiled, shaking my hand. 'Hey, thanks man. I was lucky with the three balls – if you get the three balls you are lucky. So, I buy you a drink. You are in my bar and you are my guest, so I buy you a drink. You drink beer with me?' And without waiting for my answer he loped to the bar, and returned with two huge glistening bottles of *pivo* – one in each hand – and motioned with the cigarette hanging out of his mouth to a three-legged wooden table.

'Ziveli,' he said chinking his bottle against mine.

'Ziveli.'

'By the way, my name is Kolia,' he said, offering his hand again.

'And I'm Sam.'

'So, where you from, man?'

'I'm British. English. From London. East London. Well, I say east London. It's a place called Dartford, on the border of a county… a region, called Kent. About forty minutes from London in a train. You heard of it?'

'No, man – I have not visited, I have not visited London or England.'

'OK, no worries – Dartford, where I'm from, it's where Mick Jagger grew up – you know Mick Jagger from The Rolling Stones?'

'Yes, of course – they are cool band, no? The Honky Tonk Woman, Can't Get What You Want, No Satisfaction…'

'Yes.'

He took a pull from his *pivo* and sang the opening of 'Can't

Get No Satisfaction', nodding his head, his body, to the rhythm. The German Mick Jagger. And he had a good voice. While he was singing the smoker's gravel in his throat dissolved.

He jabbed his cigarette end at me as he concluded, 'Hey, Hey, that's what I say!' He crushed his cigarette in the tin-foil ashtray with the same deprecating smile he had had after his virtuoso pinball performance.

'Hey that was good, mate. You've got a good voice.'

'Thanks, man.' The rasp was back.

'And you, where you from?

'Where am I from?'

'Yeah.'

'From here, man. From Novi Sad.'

'You're Yugoslavian?'

'Yeah, of course man. What do you think I am? This is my city. The real Novi Sad. You like it?'

'Yeah. I love the all-night bars. You know, you have this German accent when you speak English.'

'Yeah, I have lived in Berlin for some years. East Berlin.'

'Have you visited since, you know, the wall came down?'

'No, my friend, not yet. But very soon. I want to see the other side. Where all the money and girls are.' He smiles.

'But your English is fantastic.'

A slow drag of his cigarette, his right eye half-closed. 'Thanks man, but I know there are many mistakes.' Long exhalation of smoke. 'I have learnt it from the music. From your neighbour, Mick Jagger. And The Beatles. And from many others. From Bob Dylan and Jim Morrison and Bruce Springsteen and Pink Floyd and…'

'Yes, Pink Floyd. I absolutely love Pink Floyd.'

'Absolutely love Pink Floyd,' he repeated, smiling. And he knocked his bottle against mine, drained it, stood up, shouted, 'We take more beer, my friend,' and returned to the bar. I noticed that he was wearing dark brown cowboy boots.

'Ziveli.'

'Ziveli.'

'Hey, you want cigarette?'

'No thanks mate, I don't smoke – I used to, but I gave up – now only when I'm pissed.'

'*Pisst*?'

'Drunk – when I'm drunk I start smoking.'

'Pissed – that means drunk? That is same word as when you use toilet, yes? To piss?'

'Yes.'

'So, you piss in the toilet – but when you are drunk you *are* pissed? That is strange word. Like someone pisses on you.'

'Yeah. I've never really thought about it. But I suppose it can happen. When you fall over, and you're lying drunk in the street. And someone pisses on you.'

Kolia pulled on his cigarette and looked at me. 'Look, man, I tell you something, this does not happen here, in Yugoslavia – if you are lying drunk then someone helps you, man, they come and help you, help you to stand up. They do not piss on you. Never. Not here, not in Novi Sad.' He blinked his right eye as he dragged on the end of his cigarette. 'We help you, man. You understand me?'

'Hey, that's good to know, Kolia. Hope I never need that sort of help though, mate.'

'Yes, man, but if you do, we help you. We look after you

here. We are like your brothers, man. But yes, it is too cold to lie in the street tonight, no?' He smiled. 'Much better to go back to your house, I think. And where is your house, where you live here in Novi Sad? We drink beer together and I do not know why you are in my city.'

'I'm trying to play chess. In a tournament here. In the Chess Olympiad. It's sort of like the chess Olympics. They hold it every two years, and this year it's in Novi Sad.'

'That is cool, man. Very cool. Yes, I hear about this, I have friend who works there – at the Sports Hall, yes? So, you are in team for England?'

'No no, I'm not that good. They also have this side event, an open tournament that anyone can enter, and I'm playing in that.'

'Cool, man. I like that. I like to play chess also – with my friends and some beer and music. I'm not professional.'

'Yeah, but I'm not a professional either. I just play for fun.' Although probably the last time I played a game of chess for fun I was twelve years old. 'I'm still a student. A post-graduate student. I'm trying to write a PHD. On literature.'

'Yeah really? That is cool, man. I love literature also. Especially the poetry. What do you write?'

'Well, I'm writing about William Shakespeare. You know William Shakespeare?'

'Of course, man.'

'About what writers in the nineteenth century thought about him. How they were influenced by him and stuff. It's going to be called 'The Impact of Shakespeare on the Victorian Consciousness, and its Expression in their Drama, Novels and Poetry'. Or something like that.'

'OK, long title man, but that is cool. Why Shakespeare and the nineteenth century?'

'I'm not sure really… I like Shakespeare and, I don't know…

'You like the nineteenth century?'

'Yeah, I suppose so. Yeah, I do. I like some of the Victorian guys. And I suppose it seemed like a good idea a year ago…'

I didn't want to bore him with how I'd started my research by looking at Howard Staunton's work on Shakespeare but became distracted looking at his chess games again. Realising how badly he often played, how many unforced errors he made and how many of them had been glossed over by the commentators, I felt a tingle of chess creativity that I'd not felt for a long time. I put my PHD research aside to fill a notebook entitled 'Why Staunton was No Good at Chess'. I guiltily ordered Kasparov's *Test of Time* – it had come out just after I'd stopped buying new chess books. I told myself that just one book would be OK, I could handle one book. But it was the wrong book – I should have bought some utter crap by Raymond Keene. Kasparov's blazing search for chess truth pulled me away from the shadows of Shakespeare studies. Kasparov lit up the path back to the abyss and I followed willingly. No, I didn't want to bore him with all that, so I asked, 'And you, what do you do?'

'I'm a musician. I write songs and music. And play the guitar. And sing, although I'm not really a singer. I play in a band.'

'Really? That's great, what sort of music do you write? What stuff does your band do?'

'All kinds, man. Some of the covers. Like the Rolling Stones. But really we take old songs, folk songs, songs from this region, Serbia, and we do them again, we … how do you say… we do them modern?'

'You give them a modern twist?'

'Yes, exactly, the traditional Serbian folk songs and poems but with the modern music.'

'Hey, that sounds great. Really interesting.'

'Yes, I love to do this. Really. You must hear our band, Sam, we play concert in Belgrade next weekend. Start of tour for us. You are here? You come, my friend?'

'I'd love to hear your songs, but I'm going back to London the day after tomorrow.'

'Hey, but maybe you stay, my friend. Change the flight. And we meet in Belgrade next weekend? Have you already visited Belgrade? It is the best city, man. Really great city.'

Kolia stubbed out his cigarette in the ashtray. 'You know Laza Kostic, Yugoslav poet?'

I shook my head.

'No, really? OK, he is famous guy. He is one of *our* guys from nineteenth century. He was from here, from Novi Sad. We learn his poems in school. But you should know him. He loved your Shakespeare; he translated into Serb language.'

'So, you've read Shakespeare in your language, translated by this guy?'

'Yes. And he has this very famous poem that everyone knows, and we have done music for it. It is called 'Santa Maria della Salute' – you want to hear it?'

And without waiting for an answer he started singing in Serbo-Croatian, his tender voice cutting above the rumble of the pub and the jingles of the nearby pinball machine. The smoker's rasp was gone. His voice was like a freshly made cup of sweet milky tea. I couldn't understand what he was singing, but my skin could feel the beauty behind the words and the melody.

When he ended, one of the old locals who'd stopped to listen on his way back from the toilet placed a bear-like hand on Kolia's leather-jacketed shoulder and said something in Serbo-Croatian that ended in '*Brate*.' Kolia looked up at him with his self-deprecating smile. Then he fired up another cigarette.

'That was great. That sounded great. You know, it's moving, but I don't even know it means. What's it about? It sounds like a love song.'

'Yes, maybe. But it is difficult, man, difficult to translate. But it is this guy who prays to Maria… he wants the forgiveness for all the bad things he has done in his life. And how all his dreams, the ideas he had when he was young, were all bullshit. And now he realises this, and wants the forgiveness for the stupid things he has done.'

'And the guy who wrote the words, he was from Novi Sad, yes?'

'Yes, he was Serb from Novi Sad.'

'And you think the Serbs appreciate him more than other Yugoslavs?'

He took a long swig of his *pivo*. 'Maybe. But he is famous all over our country. Some crazy people say this poet is for the Serbs and this poet is for the Croats and this poet is for the Muslims, but poetry, the real poetry, is for everyone. Do you not think this?'

'Yes, absolutely. That is well said, my friend.' I tapped my bottle against his. 'Very well said. And, I hope you don't mind me asking, but it's interesting. A guy I was speaking to at the chess tournament, a Yugoslav, he was saying that there are some in the Croatian region now who are pushing for full independence from Yugoslavia. For a new country.'

'Yes, of course, this is normal. There are always people who want to destroy Yugoslavia. Break it up, you know, into the little pieces.' He took a long drag of his cigarette, his right eye closing like a sniper's. 'But it cannot happen, man. It will not happen. Yugoslavia will not let it happen.'

'Why's that?'

'Why is that? Look, you must understand something, Sam.' And he started to jab his cigarette for emphasis. 'Because we are all Yugoslavs, man. I am proud Serb, but I am also proud Yugoslav. Serbs, Croats, it is not important. We all live together. In one country. How can the Croats be independent? It is not possible – there are half a million Serbs in their region. What would happen to all these Serbs? Do they want to live in separate Croatia republic? Or must they all leave their homes and come to Belgrade? It is crazy, man. There are some crazy people, a few people with crazy heads, but the Croats are not all so stupid. No, I tell you, it will not happen.'

'But if they did? If these crazies took over and announced their independence, I don't know… enforced their independence?'

'No.' Jab of cigarette. 'It will not happen. Yugoslavia will not allow it. The Serbs will not allow it.'

'What would they do? Do you think they would fight?'

'Maybe. Probably. The army would do something. To protect the Serbs.'

'And you, would you fight?'

He looked behind, then leant forward towards me. 'I am not in the army.' And he stubbed out his cigarette slowly, looking into the ashtray as he crushed it. Then he looked up again, 'I am just musician. A simple musician. I am a lover not a fighter.' He smiled. 'And that is enough talk about politics, my friend.

It is time to talk about something else. He grinned and drained his bottle. 'But first we take more beer.'

'Hey thanks Kolia, but this one is enough for me. I'm going to have to get going soon, mate. My game starts in the morning. I need to get some sleep.'

'Yes, of course, but it is early, man. And we have not yet talked about important things, like the women. Come on man, we have one more drink together? And then we go? One more?'

The thought of my last-round match gave me a pull of tension in my stomach. But the *pivo* was blunting the serrated edges of reality and I was beginning to relax. I looked past Kolia's shoulders at the narrow pub, warmly sealed against the winter night. It was about midnight, but it was full of locals, young and old, students, workers, pensioners. And people were still pushing in through the glass door, shaking off the cold, and joining in. And no one was alone, there were no solitary drinkers, everyone was part of a group, it was like one big group, everyone leaning forward chatting and listening, or leaning back and chuckling. There was always someone laughing.
'Yeah, why not?'

'Ziveli.'
'Ziveli.'
'So, tell me something, Sam, how are the women in London? They are good, yes?'

'Yes, but I think the women here are better. You know, there are all these students working at the Olympiad in the Sports Hall. They all wear these black dresses. Like cocktail dresses. Some of them are unbelievable. Here they are students working at a chess tournament, in London they'd all be working as models.'

'You like the women in Novi Sad, Sam. You must see the women in Belgrade, my friend. In Belgrade, there are the best women in Europe. I tell you the truth. I do not say this because it is my capital. I have visited other cities – Berlin, Prague, Budapest – but Belgrade is the best. You know, man, whenever I go to Belgrade I cannot stop looking at all these women. I fall in love a hundred times in Belgrade.'

'That could be a pop song. 'In Belgrade I fall in love a hundred times'.'

'Yes, man, I like that. Maybe, I will write this song. And you will translate into English for me, yes?' And he smoked and nodded, thinking about lines or a melody for the song, or about the beautiful women. 'You must go to Belgrade and see. You must change flight.'

I had nothing to go back to London for. There was no one waiting for me there, only my cracked pocket chess set in the dark empty flat. 'Maybe I will. I wouldn't want to miss your band. Or the women.'

He raised his bottle to me. 'But you must, Sam. You must see Belgrade. And you, Sam, you have someone in London?'

'Well, not at the moment. I used to, but she left me. In the summer.'

'That is bad, my friend. She left you? Sorry to hear this. And she was beautiful?'

'Well, I think so. To me. Yes, she was, she is.'

'And you love this woman?'

'Yes, I did. I do.'

'Then why has she left you?'

'I don't know really. Well, I do know. I wasn't spending enough time with her. To be completely honest, I was playing too much chess.'

'You were playing too much chess?'

'Yes.'

'So, you have beautiful woman and you love her, and you leave her to play chess?'

'Yes.'

He shook his head, then swept some strands of his vinyl-black hair away from his eyes. 'Chess is good game, man, I like to play with friends. But it is not life my friend. The women are life, Sam, the love is life. Maybe I should not say this – I say it because you are my friend – but you are crazy guy.'

'Yes, you're right. It was a bit crazy, I am a bit crazy. And to be honest I still feel bad about it. She's a great person, Kolia. And she did nothing wrong, apart from loving me. And I pushed her away.'

'Look, Sam, we all make the mistakes. Especially with the women. I have made many mistakes with the women. Too many. But you can change things. I know this also. It is like the poem by Laza Kostic, like our song, you make the mistakes, but then you realise, and you ask for the forgiveness. You must speak to her, Sam, tell her that you made mistake.'

'Yes, maybe I should. But it's not that easy. I haven't spoken to her since she left me. And then she left England. She's in Germany now, in Berlin, at a university in the West somewhere. I think maybe she stayed there because of me…'

'England, Germany, Yugoslavia – it does not matter, my friend – the world is much smaller than love. If you love her, you will find her. Look, I tell you something – after Belgrade, we, my band, go to Germany, to Berlin for some concerts, small concerts. We know lots of guys in Berlin. We go in my friend's bus, small bus, but you come with us, we take you with us, and you can go through the wall, and you see your girlfriend there.'

'No, that's crazy…'

'It is not crazy – love is most important thing man. I learn one thing in life Sam – everything is about love. You should go through the wall, Sam, and find your girlfriend.'

'I'm not even sure that foreigners can cross over from the East, can they?'

'The wall is finished, man. You will find a way. You know that Shakespeare says the walls do not stop love.'

'Does he?'

'Yes, in *Romeo and Julia*.'

'Which character says that?'

'Romeo says it. This is line in one of our songs. Romeo knew this.'

'Ah yes, that's right, you're right. Romeo says 'walls cannot hold love out'. Yes, that's true. That's very good, Kolia. You know Shakespeare better than me and I've not even heard of your poet.'

He pulled on his *pivo* and winked at me. 'OK, so you come with us?'

'I'm not sure, it'll be difficult, but yeah maybe I could… maybe I should.'

'Of course, Sam. And when you find her, tell her you love her more than the chess.' He sucked in smoke and grinned at me.

I smiled. 'Yes, I will.'

'And we must drink to that, Sam. But we need more beer.' He jumped up.

'Hey Kolia, no more for me, mate, I need to go and get some sleep.'

'Hey, it's early man.'

'Yeh, but I've got a big game tomorrow.' And for the first time there was no apprehension thinking about the match the next day; the *pivo* had untied the knot in my stomach.

'But we must drink to you and your girlfriend. What is her name?'

'Lauren.'

'To Sam and Lauren. And your happy life together.'

'Sorry Kolia, it's time for me to go, I can't drink any more beer – I'm already feeling a bit drunk.'

'You are *pisst*, yes?'

'Yes, I think I am, a bit. It's this Yugoslav beer, it's strong stuff.' Kolia had perhaps begun to gesticulate more elaborately with his cigarette hand, but otherwise he seemed unaffected by all the *pivo* we'd drunk.

'OK, man, *keine Sorge*, no worries, yes, you must sleep, and you must win tomorrow. I will come to the Sports Hall tomorrow to support you.'

'Hey thanks mate, that would be great. Although I'm playing another Yugoslav, one of your countrymen. You still want to support the crazy English guy?'

'It doesn't matter to me, man. I support the guy I drink with. I support my friend.'

I chinked my nearly-empty bottle against his empty bottle. 'And now I'm sorry to say I must go. Give me your phone number, mate.'

'OK, man. It was good to meet you. But I tell you one thing. It is tradition here, big tradition, to drink one *slivovitz*, before you leave. You know *slivovitz*?'

'No, mate, what is it?'

'You do not know *slivovitz*? It is famous drink in my country – it is made from… I don't know word in English… but it is small fruit. You must try it, Sam, before you go.'

'Is it alcoholic?'

'Yes, it is alcoholic. But it is very small, and it is very good for the health, it will warm you for your journey. Also, the *slivovitz* will help you sleep. Just one and then we go.'

'Ziveli.'

'Ziveli.'

He upended the colourless jam-smelling liquid into his mouth. I copied him and a mix of Um Bongo Juice and petrol ignited my throat and chest.

I coughed, my eyes watering.

'You like it, man?'

'…'

'It's good, yes?'

'…'

'You get used to it, man.' And he was looking at me and he started laughing, and when the coughing stopped I was laughing as well, my eyes watering even more.

On the way out he stopped at a table with two of his friends (two female students – one in a maroon bobble hat, one in a black beret) and introduced me. 'This is my friend Sam and he is from England, from London, and his neighbour is Mick Jagger in The Rolling Stones, and he plays chess here at the Sports Hall, and he loves Pink Floyd, absolutely loves Pink

Floyd, and he writes about Shakespeare, and he is going to translate a song for me into English, and he will visit Belgrade next week for my concert, and then come with us to Berlin to see his girlfriend. Yes, Sam?'

And we drank another *slivovitz* with them (I was ready for it this time and avoided the coughing fit). And the older guy with the big hands who'd stopped earlier to listen to Kolia sing joined us and we had another *slivovitz* (a bottle had appeared on the table). There was joking and laughing in Serbo-Croatian which I was beginning to understand. Then one of his musician friends sat with us (wearing a Springsteen denim waist-coat) and we had another *slivovitz*. And we had one more *slivovitz* to wish me luck in my game tomorrow (the two students had left, two of Kolia's other mates had replaced them), and we had a last one to help me sleep.

When Kolia and I finally stepped outside it was snowing, invisible except for the flakes whirling around a lonely street lamp. Beyond that was the mighty dark river. It was scrotum-tighteningly cold, although the *slivovitz* was protecting me like a luxurious body warmer.

'Hey, Sam, good luck man. It was cool to meet you and to drink with you, really cool.'

I was swaying like a sapling in the wind. 'Hey right, man, thanks, man, for all the drinks and the *shlivovitch* – it's great, man.'

'I give you my number, man. You have pen?'

I threw down my cigarette and spent five minutes digging my Parker out of the jacket pocket and he wrote on the ripped off top of his cigarette packet: 'Kolia, Novi Sad – 650022'.

'You give me call anytime, man.'

'Yes, I will, definitely. And you come to the chess tomorrow?'

'Yes, I'll be there, man. And I'll see you in Belgrade.'

'Yes, Belgrade, Belgrade city where the girls are pretty, I'll be there, man.'

'And then to Berlin?'

'And then to Berlin. And through the wall. I'll be there.'

I offered him my hand but he went for the continental bear hug.

'You'll be OK going back?' he asked.

'Yes man, A-OK, absolutely A-OK,'

Off I went and slipped over, breaking the fall with my right arm on the snow, my right cheek resting on its soothing wetness.

'Hey, man, are you OK?' He came over to help, to pick me up, but I didn't need his help, springing up like a prize fighter who never goes down.

'Yes, yes, no problem man, someone left some snow lying down there,' I said brushing down my leather jacket.

And I was off again.

'Hey Sam,' he called. I turned unsteadily. 'You do one thing. Make sure that you find Laura.'

I watched him as he walked backwards down the street, fading into the snow.

'Yes, I will,' I shouted back and gave him a thumbs-up, but I couldn't see him anymore.

9

Ah, here we go, the Yugoslav is stirring – we're going to get some action. He takes the mangled end of his pen out of his mouth. He scratches his head, he rubs his black stubbly chin, he looks at his clock…

Chess Time: White: 53 minutes
Black: 47 minutes

He gurns like a gargoyle, scratches his head again, and pulls his bishop back to add cover to the kingside.

And that's the best way to do it. In the Rubik's Cube reshuffling of the kingside it's best to click that bishop back first. Maybe this guy is no idiot. It took me an afternoon to realise that's the most accurate move, and he's found it in a few minutes, but it's easier to find when your life depends on it.

I take a calming sip of my coffee – ah, that's good. Now should I spring out my move quickly or have a pretend think? I don't like to do anything fake in chess. I follow Fischer's dictum that you don't need psychology in chess, just good moves. Lies and hypocrisy don't exist on the chessboard. So, I heave my knight further forward, and screw it into its new outpost. That move is the truth, my friend.

The Yugoslav looks at my no-bull knight snorting in front of his king's pawns, and pulls his own knight to the back rank – on its way to shore up the kingside. That was the knight that I kept forgetting to adjust; well it doesn't matter now… although it doesn't look fully on its square there either… let me see… well its whole base is in the square, although only about a millimetre away from the edge, so it could be adjusted, but let's not worry about it – I'm still in my preparation so it's not going to affect my concentration.

I'm punching forward, he's scrambling backwards. All moves I'd predicted on my pocket set last month, but on move 25 he slides his king into the corner square, not with his pinkie but with his chubby index finger. The king jigging to the right before the missiles start pouring in. I didn't consider that one. I was just looking at ways he could rearrange his pieces. But is it any good? Why move the king? When the king's castle walls disintegrate will the corner be a safer or a more perilous place? How can anyone know at this stage? However, I'm encouraged by the huge geometric distance that now exists between the white king and the white queen – his consort is miles away, lazing on my corner square, doing nothing, guiltily digesting my queen's rook.

And that's it, I finally have an original position in front of me – my pocket set, resting on the coffee table back in London, never saw this one. Or did I leave it on the arm of the settee?

Anyway, I'm on my own now. The boat has slipped away from its mooring.

OK, time to take stock:

Material – Rook and two pawns down.

Queenside – Game Over.

Kingside – Big attacking chances for me. An immense knight hovering near his king's position. Queen lurking with murderous intent.

Time Situation – Fifty-five minutes gone for him; nearly fifty minutes gone for me. He's finally overtaken me, although I've used fifty minutes and haven't even made an original move. Need to work on my time management.

Mental states – Psychological advantage to me. The Yugoslav is definitely all over the place. Stunned by my novelty he's now staring down the barrel of a kingside attack, whereas I'm only just out of my preparation, and ready for action. But I'm a rook down.

Physical states – I don't know about the Yugoslav, but my hangover has nearly gone, washed out by the caffeine, adrenalin and time. My mouth feels better and the pain in my right arm has faded. Although, I'm going to need the toilet soon.

First however, I need to have a think about this position. It's time to start working, time to earn my second place. Time to start creating.

We're rapidly approaching the Critical Position, when all my attacking forces will be in their optimal positions, straining to throw themselves at the white king. And soon the Yugoslav will have set up his optimal defensive position. So, I've got to break through. One of my pieces will have to detonate himself to breach the white king's defences. Because if I don't smash through, the Yugoslav will consolidate and I'm just a rook down – game over.

I need to sacrifice something and soon. Probably now. I can sacrifice either my queen's bishop waiting in his starting blocks on the queenside or my super-knight on his kingside redoubt. But which one? Bishop or knight?

Decision time. This is what chess is – a sequence of decisions. That is what a chess player is – a decision-maker. The best decision-maker wins the game. But then I suppose that's what life is – a sequence of decisions. All the time, trying to make the right decision – tea or coffee, get drunk or stay sober, leave your girlfriend or stick with her, give up on love or work it out... bishop or knight?

And how to make that right decision? How do you know whether to take the main road or the less-travelled one? The decision that will improve your position – or your life? You have to put your head in your hands and work it out, that's how. You have to think like a grandmaster. You have to analyse each option objectively and weigh up the one that brings about the biggest advantage. And hope that somehow you unearth the truth...

Bishop or knight? I always start by analysing the move that I *want* to play, the move that my gut is telling me to play. Often your gut is right, but you need your head to double-check it. Reason as the slave to your passions and all that. The piece that my tingling fingers want to grab is that bishop on the queenside, straining like a greyhound in the slips. In the King's Indian that bishop has only one mission in life – to martyr himself on White's kingside – headlong into that pawn on h3 – crunch! And that steely bishop looks ready. My right hand has made that move so many times in blitz and analysis that I have to hide it between my sticky thighs in case it flashes out the move before my brain orders it to do so.

Need to concentrate. Time to calculate some variations. Need to stop thinking about coffee, my bubbling stomach, Kolia, Berlin, Lauren, and *concentrate*. But first I need to sort that off-centre white knight. You can't work on a complicated position like this with a piece not fully on its square. I extend my arm out over the board to adjust the knight and my opponent's dark eyes widen from stolid contemplation to alarm – why is the English guy's hand in my position, have I missed something, is he taking off one of my pieces? When he realises what I am doing his eyes contemptuously resume their steady focus on the position. I feel bad about scaring him like that, but that knight was annoying me. Can't concentrate with a piece higgledy-piggledy on its square.

OK, now I can get to work: bishop takes pawn on h3, pawn takes, queen up.... to my right there is a susurration of voices as two players down on Board 6 or 7 finish their game. Shut up, will you? I'm trying to concentrate over here. The grey-haired chief arbiter lopes to their board and stoops over to take control of the post-game practicalities – clock stopping, score-sheet signing, piece resetting – his school-masterly presence ends their talking.

So, bishop takes pawn on h3, pawn takes, queen up, knight to f2... now what? The Tooth-Fairy makes a move on Board 4. He's thrown another piece into Black's kingside and is relaxing in his chair like a spider who's just finished wrapping a fly. There are now more Black pieces than White pieces in Animal's king's position. He's going to need a miracle to survive that one...

But I need to concentrate on *my* position ... so, what to play after his knight to f2? What have I got there? Need to get my queen in to give a check, but how? All his pieces are defending everything. And he's still chewing on his pen. The baby with his dummy. That's really irritating. Maybe I should tell him. But what would I say to him? 'Sorry, mate, could you stop chewing your pen? It's annoying me, I know it's not making any noise but it's the sort of thing that could make noise so please stop…'

Come on Sam, must block everything out.

I cradle my head in my hands using them as blinkers and plug my thumbs into my ears, big James Howell style – muffled tunnel vision towards the chessboard. No sound, no time, only the blood pumping in my ears. Bishop takes pawn, pawn takes, queen up…

I awake from my calculations some time later (minutes or a lifetime?), the possessor of new knowledge: the bishop sacrifice doesn't work. My gut was wrong. I've tried all the attacking tricks over there – rook lift, knight jiggle, even the quiet queen retreat – and I'm not getting in to his king, he's holding everything together.

Time to move on to the knight sacrifice – that's the one my brain's telling me to play but my gut is telling me not to give up that knight on f4; it's too strong, it's as potent as a rook up there, more than a rook, it's an archbishop, a chancellor. But, as always, some clinical calculation is needed to see whether my gut is talking crap.

I look up at the high windows, fill my lungs with air, take a last pull of my coffee cup, upending it over my nose to dribble the sugary dregs into my mouth – a human aardvark with a big white snout. Andic is staring over at me, the trace of a frown on his forehead, and I quickly take the cup out of my mouth, rest it on the table, and hunker back down into the tunnel…

Knight takes pawn on h3, pawn takes knight, queen up… and a fragment of dream from last night's drunken sleep flashes up. Someone giving me a copy of Kasparov's *Test of Time*, a pale hand leaning into my vision with the book, but it has a different cover: not that sepia photo of young Garry in his tennis shirt and winner's smirk. There's no photo – the book's cover is shiny black with 'Test of Time' written across the middle in blood red lettering. And that's it, I can't remember anything else. Who was giving me the book? Who's hand was it? Lauren's? Kasparov's? My opponent's? My father's? And why were they giving me it? And does that edition with a black cover even exist … have I seen it somewhere? And why am I remembering that dream now as I look at knight takes h3? Why didn't the memory of the dream come to me when I was draining my coffee, or looking at bishop takes h3, or on the public bus this morning? Maybe I sacrificed a knight later in the dream. I can't remember. I scrabble around the edges, trying to look beyond the hand to the person, but I can't see any further. Could this be an omen, the spirit of Kasparov come to me from Lyons, telling me that knight takes pawn is the right move?

No, I don't believe in omens, I believe in brute force calculation…

And, I realise that this time my gut was right – the knight sacrifice also doesn't work. I just don't have enough firepower to follow up either sacrifice. It's too early for a sacrifice… but soon it will be too late. Very soon. We are hitting the Critical Moment. And you've got to get it right. The timing. And my stomach is also hitting a Critical Moment. I feel a gentle loosening of the bowels. All that *pivo* and *slivovitz* and burger and coffee pushing for release.

But first I must make a move. If neither of the sacrifices are working then what can I do? I'm at maximum capacity over there. All my pieces are on their optimal squares. What can I do? What can I do here? Bring my king up to join in the attack? Has the Yugoslav's king sidestep taken all the air out of my attack? Is that it, the refutation of the Patrick Moore Variation, my rook sacrifice novelty?

Surely one of these sacrifices works. Bishop or knight. I chunk through the variations again but uncover nothing new, not one alternative move or idea – I spend time just confirming what I already know, and realising this brings about another jolt of the bowels. I pray to God that I don't soil myself here and now at the board in the middle of the tournament hall.

I look up and zone in on the high windows – the sky's earlier metallic sheen replaced by dark fungal clouds – composing myself. Breathe in, breathe out. Clench the buttocks.

Chess Time: White: 1 hour 1 minute
Black: 1 hour 2 minutes

It's no use, I'm going to have go with my clock ticking…

10

At the exit, I turn left down the cool corridor rather than right to the commerce of the coffee station. The toilets are in the large changing rooms – wooden slatted benches, rough tiled floor, banks of red aluminium lockers, all their doors shut apart from one. A window is open somewhere letting in a thrilling breeze. The chlorine tang of bleach isn't fully blocking out the seaweedy odour emanating from the line of toilet cubicles at the far end.

Fantastic – a free cubicle. Thank you, God. My toxic stomach is pushing down heavily as I kick open the door.

On the cool cuckstool I bend forward, elbows on bare legs, head in hands, staring at the pimply grey-tiled floor. Clearing my gut and mind. I can use the time here to think about my position, how I'm going to break through. The tiles are chessboard squares. But I don't need them – I can bring the position up in my mind's eye. Ah, there it is, sharp and restored on the screen of my brain. Not like Nabokov's grandmaster in his novel *The Luzhin Defense* who imagines a mating attack up the h-file of the toilet pipes.

There is a Serbo-Croatian cough from someone outside the stalls.

Poor Luzhin. I loved that book when I first read it at school and still go back to it. The chess world is better, life is better, because Nabokov created that work of art. I wish James Joyce had also written about chess, the great Leopold Bloom musing on the game as he wanders around Dublin. As I wish Shakespeare had written one of his sonnets on chess. His only chess depiction is that strange game between Miranda and Ferdinand in *The Tempest* where she accuses him of cheating but when he denies it she says she doesn't care, she wants him to cheat against her. Little minx. But for poetry there is John Fuller's masterpiece about Staunton's refusal to play Morphy, when the Englishman went back to working on his Shakespeare editions rather than take his beating from the young American. I can't remember what Staunton himself wrote about Miranda's chess game – I'll have to check that in the library when I get back...

A cubicle door slams to my right.

And there's that other classic novel, or novella, by Stefan Zweig, *Chess Story*. Poor Zweig. World-tired by the persecution of the Jews in Europe and his own exile, he called it a day in 1941 or 1942, although of course he didn't know the half of it. He played some chess during that final exile in Brazil, although I'm not sure he understood the game like Nabokov did. For Zweig it remained a metaphor, whereas Nabokov was also able to depict the grainy realities of being a chess player. Nabokov who regretted all the time he spent composing chess problems because it took him away from his verbal adventures.

But writing literature about chess is hard. How to render the sublimity of chess in words? You start by using the language of battle – infantry marching up the board, cavalry charges on the kingside, artillery pounding from the back rank. Then you try to breathe life into the pieces, anthropomorphise them, so that the pawns are humble serfs, the knights Arthurian warriors, the bishops crafty clerics, the queen like Lady Macbeth. You can also compare chess to other artistic endeavors: the visual combination as a painting; the king hunt as poetry; Nabokov describes a whole game as a symphony. But ultimately, I suppose, words fail. And you realise that the only thing that can describe chess is chess itself, only the moves themselves can depict its ineffable beauty.

It sounds like someone's dropped a boot into one of the toilet bowls to my right or left.

But how are chess players depicted in these fictions? In both novels, and Fuller's poem, chess brings about a certain order in the lives of the heroes but ultimately it fails them and leads to disappointment and/or madness. Chess as a metaphor for the rejection of life. But what about chess as a celebration of life – a novel showing the chess player as an artist and chess playing as a surpassing experience, a worthwhile attainment with the capacity to enrich life?

A toilet flushes, water whirls and gurgles.

Chess is like life, as Spassky said.

From its mewling opening full of possibilities and hope, through its middle-game of adventure and critical decisions, to its lean endgame where you harvest success or failure. And regardless of how it ends, win or lose, the clocks are stopped, the pieces are packed away, and the coffin lid of the chess box is closed.

Chess *is* life, as Fischer said.

11

I bounce back into the tournament hall, feeling lighter – my poisoned stomach removed. Back into action. I wish I'd spent more time thinking about my position in the toilets, but I'm confident that I'll find a way through to the Yugoslav's king.

Chess Time: White: 1 hour 1 minute
Black: 1 hour 16 minutes

Good, only fifteen minutes or so lost to my comfort break.
The full gang are around me. Hello, everyone – I'm back. The German kid, Antic, Pavlovic aka the Toothy-Fairy, Animal, and my Yugoslav, all looking down at the boards – calculating, decision-making, solving, trying to make things work. And afterwards, mentally battered, we'll sit down together in the analysis room and have a chat, compare notes about our experiences, like those documentaries where old foes meet up years later – the Argentinian having a beer with a Welsh guardsman.
The Yugoslav and I are locked in this together – it is with him that I must struggle through this day. Till what? Till he yields to me.

We're both calculating sacrifices, but, whereas I'm trying to make them work, he must ensure that they don't. And he has to see them all, I only have to find one. The pressure of the defender. Those teddy-bear dark eyes, peering out from those chubby eye sockets, working manically on the kingside.

This is it, guys – we're at the Critical Position. The box shuts next move. I've got to find something here. Or resign…

…but I can't do it. I can't find the answer. If there even is an answer. And my head is hurting again, a hair-line crack of a headache on the top of my head. I'm not good enough. Philip Roth wrote somewhere (in a forward?) that if you want to be reminded of your limitations you should become a writer – your memory, intelligence, and understanding will never be enough. I say you should become a chess player – then you'll find out what's missing in you.

But maybe there just isn't anything for Black here. Maybe Black is just lost – sans queen's rook and sans attack. But my gut, my intuition, my chess senses, wired from thousands of hours spent playing through thousands of history's games, are telling me that Black has something. I just need to find it. But what else can I sacrifice? My rook? My queen? My king?

Head in hands, I cover my eyes with my palms to see things more clearly. I go through all the attacking possibilities, thrashing around like a fish in an empty bucket. I can't see anything. I'm pushing my palms deeper into my eye sockets. But his kingside will not give way. Until finally, thank you God, heels of my palms squashing down my eyes, I see a long winding line that ends in a resounding checkmate delivered by my rook. The adrenalin swabs my body before I realise that my rook came off the board at the start of the variation.

And that's it. It's time to admit defeat. I can connect nothing with nothing.

I look up, my eyes sore, blue and red shrimps bobbing in front of me, and a horrible wave of unreality hits me – a slab of panic in my stomach. Who am I? What am I doing here? *Why* am I here?

Then I see my father. He's not looking at my game but at Board 1, standing behind the young Latvian playing there. He's wearing his dark shiny suit, no tie, but it's too big for him. The grey-coloured wiry wings are there on either side of his otherwise hairless head. And he looks ill. God, what are you doing here? My stomach is pumping out pure panic.

The shrimps fade and the sepia haze clears, and I see that it is not my father but Mikhail Tal. The magician from Riga. Who spanked the young Fischer four out of four in the Candidates in Yugoslavia in 1959 on his way to becoming World Champion. And there he is standing a few feet away from me, come down from his mountain kingdom to look at how one of his protégés is doing. He'd be playing himself next door in the Olympiad, rather than just spectating and commentating, if they'd let Latvia join the party, getting stuck in alongside their young guns, Shirov and Shabalov. Although, he doesn't look too good – he looks worse than I did when I got up this morning – his health burnt through by cigarettes, booze and blitz. Nothing left of those fearsome good looks that stare out at you from the covers of his books. Now, it looks like every third thought is of the grave. Although he's still the magician, he's not broken his staff yet, and could beat anyone in the world.

What is he seeing over there on Board 1? What would he see in my position? Would he be able to conjure something here with Black? What would Tal play? I spent that entire Christmas holiday trying to find out what Tal would play while working through *Study Chess with Tal*. It was a darkly cold winter, and I stayed in bed most of the time in football socks, pyjamas, three jumpers, and bobble hat, as if I were ill, but I was studying chess with Tal, cross-hatching every page of the book with pencilled notes and variations. I got in the soup when I returned to school because I hadn't done the holiday maths homework – I'd spent twelve hours a day for three weeks filling a book with chess variations but I couldn't spare an hour to solve some algebra questions. But it was a dangerous book for an impressionable teenager – in every game for the next few months I was sacrificing something, usually without justification and certainly without Tal's savage calculating ability.

Suddenly Tal turns and looks at me staring at him. And the cold dark eyes haven't changed, they're the same eyes that chilled the young Bobby four times in 1959. And I immediately look away, up at the high windows, at the softer eyes of my opponent. And Tal shuffles away down the boards, the frayed sleeves of his suit jacket almost covering his hands – his wizard's cloak – and out of our tournament hall, away from this insubstantial pageant, back towards the Olympiad playing hall.

What *would* Tal play here? When I'm stuck for ideas, I often ask myself what Kasparov would do, and it can give a more dynamic perspective on the position. It's the same when I'm writing – I ask myself what would Joyce do? And if I'm going nowhere I put the chessboard or notebook aside, and I read through some *Test of Time* or some *Ulysses* to hear them, those imperial voices falling on me like an enormous yes.

What *would* Tal play here? Bishop or knight? But that wouldn't be the question for Tal. He would just sacrifice. He would sacrifice both bishop and knight, and then everything else and mate you with a pawn. Bishop and knight…

Bishop *and* knight. Christ, what's that? Why didn't I consider that? Bishop *and* knight. Do both. Both gut *and* brain. I thought I'd looked at everything. I need to look at that. How much time have I got left?

Chess time: White: 1 hour 1 minute
Black: 1 hour 24 minutes

Thirty-five minutes left. Where's all my time going? Can someone stop time for a bit so that I can work all this out?

And the heavy head goes back onto the pedestal of the sweaty hands and the thumbs slot back in the ears, and the sorcerer's apprentice starts clattering through the variations after the bishop *and* knight sacrifice.

I'm encouraged by a line where I'm cracking open his king. With some excitement I see a variation that leads to a draw by perpetual check – the first variation I've looked at for a long time that doesn't lose.

Then I see something beautiful. Truly beautiful. In one line after the bishop and knight sacrifices, I can sacrifice my rook to winkle out his king, queen-check him up the board, sacrifice my queen, and then checkmate him with my knight. Jesus, that's good. Sometimes chess is just too good. I want to jump up and show the variation to the gang – look guys, look what I've just seen – there is something heart-stoppingly beautiful here. Imagine if I could finish the game like that... 'Renshawe demonstrates a Tal-like finish to take second place in the Novi Sad Open.'

But let me look at that again. Have I missed something? No, that variation works out – it's true. Jesus, that's good.

Hold on, I'm getting too excited here. I need to calm down. My hands are forming a poker visor over my face so he can't see me, but I need to ease my breathing. I need to look at these variations again. Check everything. Stay objective. Don't let the creative juices wash away the objective analysis. That's just one fantasy line. He has a lot of other defensive possibilities after the knight and bishop sacrifices.

I put in more head-hurting brain work. The more I see, the better it looks. I'm in a cake shop and everywhere I look I see something better than before ... there's a check, there's a big fork, there's a deadly skewer, and there's a fat, mouth-watering checkmate.

Sweet Lord, after the bishop and knight sacrifice my attack seems to be seeping through. Everything is rhyming, everything is working out, I'm connecting everything with everything...

'Hey, you see that little shelter over there, above the beach, that's where T. S. Eliot wrote some of *The Waste Land*.'

Lauren turned her gaze from the sunset over the sea to the front. 'Really? You mean that little thing that looks like a bus shelter? Where that man's dog's having a wee?'

'Yep, he's pissing in the very spot where Eliot wrote 'On Margate Sands I can connect nothing with nothing.' He was having a breakdown and came to Margate to get away from his wife.'

'Who? The dog or Eliot?'

'Both.'

'Well, I hope you never come here to sit in a bus shelter to get away from me,' she said, poking me in the ribs.

'Never! With you on Margate Sands I can connect everything with everything.'

'Well, darling, that's terribly nice of you to say so,' she said in her Virginia Woolf voice. 'You're the real expert on Margate aren't you? And what other interesting facts do you have for me?'

'Mmm, let me see... well, over there near Eliot's shelter there was this old wooden kiosk where we used to get our ice creams – always a 99 with a flake. I always wanted candy floss but my dad would never let me, it had to be an ice cream. And see just up there, near those rocks, that was my dad's favourite place to sit on the beach. He'd be angry all day if anyone got there first. Always in a deck-chair. He'd take off his socks and shoes – and I do mean shoes, black shoes – and his shirt, and sit there all day in his trousers.'

'What, even if it was baking hot?'

'Yep, whatever the temperature. I don't think he ever owned a pair of shorts. And read his paper from the back to the front and then again from the front to the back. Sometimes even with a handkerchief on his head, like one of those cartoons on a postcard.'

'Noooo! Really?'

'Yes, really. That was his way of keeping the sun of his bald head. I'm not sure why he never bought a hat...'

'And what was little Sam doing while his dad was sitting in his deck-chair?'

'You know, with no brothers or sisters there wasn't so much to do, I suppose. I did a lot of reading. Chess books mostly. I was big into chess in those days. I used to sit on the sand with a pocket chess set and a book.'

'A bit of a chess geek, weren't you?' she said poking me in the ribs again.

'Ouch. Yes, I suppose I was. But at least I wasn't in love with my horse.'

'I never said I was in love with my horse – but I did used to talk to him a lot… and at least I was outdoors in the open air.'

'So was I, but I was talking to my pocket set. And see that amusement park lit up over there? That's the famous Dreamland, a necessary part of any visit to Margate. It's tacky but… I'll take you there tomorrow morning before we go back.'

'Wow, really? You do know how to treat a lady.'

'Yes, but only if you behave yourself. I remember this one afternoon when my dad wanted us all to go to Dreamland, but I wanted to go and find this hotel instead where there'd been a famous chess tournament in the thirties and he got really pissed off about it for some reason. But way over the top – I mean just because I didn't want to go to Dreamland.'

We continued walking along the beach, hand in hand, in the cool autumn air with its waft of fish and chips, salt and vinegar.

'You know that Russian-American writer, Vladimir Nabokov?'

'He's the one who wrote *Lolita*, right? I keep meaning to read it. Abigail read it and said it was weird but good.'

'Yep… well, he also wrote this novel, one of his early novels in Russian, about a chess player, called Luzhin. At the start, he writes about Luzhin's father. The father thinks he has this very gifted son but is worried because he's solitary, morose, non-communicative, that sort of thing. But his father has these fantasies that his son will eventually become a great poet or musician or something. But instead the son finds chess. At the start the father is excited that his son is finally interested in something and has an outlet for his natural gifts, but when all his son does is play chess to the exclusion of everything else, he becomes disappointed and feels that his son is wasting his talents and time… the father finds it harder and harder to be proud of his achievements. I think it was a bit like that with my dad. Not as extreme of course, and I was very far from being a prodigy or anything, but I think there was some of that. I think he sort of felt… I don't know… let down. Thought I should be doing something a bit more worthwhile.'

Lauren gripped my arm. 'I'm sure that can't be true. I'm sure he was very proud of the stuff you did.'

'I don't know. Probably. I think he would be now. If he could have seen that I'd got my degree and was doing a PHD and stuff. And could meet you.' I squeezed her arm back. 'But back then I just lost interest in everything, except for playing chess. I'm not sure why really. And a part of me thinks he was a bit disappointed with it, with me.'

We stopped again to gaze at the sunset – a red orange beach ball sinking into the sea's horizon from a darkening grey-blue sky, streaked above by mauve clouds like tyre tracks. The waves were sighing against the sand with their eternal note of sadness.

She brushed my cheek with a kiss, and let go of my hand and danced away from me, her long legs as delicate as a crane's, her shoulder blades exposed beneath the straps of her dress, like incipient angel wings, and I knew that if I was much closer, lying next to her, I would see the microscopic fine blonde hairs that ran down her spine. She turned around and, dancing to silent music, looked at me, smiling. That electrifying face-changing smile. When that smile was turned on you it was more beautiful than any sunset, any Kasparov combination, any line of Shakespeare.

As I looked at her in her pink DMs and floral dress, her black sweater tied around her waist, swaying to invisible music in the fading light, I was suddenly struck by the terrible reality that this beautiful life force would one day end. And I felt an ineffable sadness. I walked forward and held her.

'Hey, Sam, are you OK?'

'Yes, yes,' I said into the clean cool skin of her shoulder. 'It's just that I don't know... I love you and I want to tell you that nothing bad will ever happen to you while I'm with you.'

'Hey, that's a beautiful thing to say, Sam... and I love you too.'

More than half the huge blood-orange sun was in the sea.

And she broke off our embrace to pick up a small rock with which she energetically engraved into the sand: 'Sam and Lauren for ever'. Then she added a big fat heart.

'What do you think of my artwork?'

'It's nice. Although you know that the sea is coming up. It'll wipe that away soon.'

She pouted. 'Sometimes you say the strangest things. Sometimes you think too much, Sammy. It doesn't matter that it'll be gone soon, just enjoy it while it's there.'

'Yes, sorry, I mean that I like it so much that I want it to be permanent... I don't know... it's just I don't like the idea of things ending.'

'Nothing's going to end, stupid. And, I think you should

see it as an artistic paradox – the physical form will disappear, but the spiritual reality of our love will continue.'

The sun was a tangerine ember hovering above the horizon.

'And as you want something more permanent I think it's time for me to give you your holiday present,' she said, and pulled a small paper bag out of her dress pocket.

'What is it?'

'Open it and see.'

It was a key ring with a squidgy white rubber rook attached to it.

'I saw it in that gift shop and thought of you.'

I smiled. 'I'll keep it with me wherever I go. It'll be my lucky Lauren talisman.' I kissed her beautiful mouth, and squeezed my rubber rook, and felt part of life.

Everything is working out. All the variations are connecting. I'm not even sure what the Yugoslav can do to stay on the board after the bishop and knight sacrifices. What a turnaround! I'm now looking for ways for *him* to avoid losing, and I'm struggling to find anything. Surely there must be something for him? He'll be a rook, bishop and knight up…

But there's nothing – even with all his treasure he can't defend his king.

I love the King's Indian. I'm going to devote myself to it for the rest of my life… I'm going to write a book on it, *the* book on it, a solid Batsford hardback, not one of those new flexicover efforts… and I'll put this game in the introduction – 'It was my last round win against Mitrovic in the Novi Sad Open in 1990, employing for the first time the so-called Patrick Moore Sacrifice that inspired me to write this book. This game, which will repay the reader's careful study, is a model example of Black's dynamic chances against White's monarch, even allowing for a considerable deficit in material.'

Deep breath. OK, this is it. Time to go off the high-board. Time to grab the critical moment. What is the time now? Not real time, but chess time? I don't care about real time.

Chess time: White: 1 hour 1 minute
*   Black: 1 hour 36 minutes.*

Over one and a half hours gone. Not counting my toilet break, I spent about half an hour working all that out. It felt like a couple of minutes. The relativity of chess time. But it was worth it. Although with less than thirty minutes left I'm going to have to stay at the board, stop my walkabouts, sit on my hands. I'd like another coffee but I'm going to have to wait. As my dad used to say, *You can't always have what you want, son.*

Writing down the move – Bxh3 – my hand is trembling at the prospect of what I'm about to do. My score sheet is a mess. Most of the moves are indecipherable Arabic scrawls. There are thumbprints and sweat stains all over it – even a coffee ring at the top over the Novi Sad Olympiad logo: a black rook with a white bird flying over it – an appropriate emblem for the Patrick Moore Sacrifice.

I breathe in deeply. Some moves change the rest of your life. This is one of them. Here we go…

I flex out my sweaty right hand, grab my bishop and longleap him over to the kingside where he disintegrates the white pawn with a resonant plastic click.

The bishop stands on the fatal square, bending up to his full height.

I press down on the cold button of my clock.

I will show this Yugoslav how to war.

12

How beautiful that black bishop looks on h3, nobly awaiting his execution. The beauty of the martyr. Sebastian with his head held high before the arrows strike.

The Yugoslav's eyes are also fixed on that bishop. But what is he thinking about him? You've always got to consider what the other guy is thinking. There was this Scottish player at the British Championships in Eastbourne who would regularly go to the other side of the board to see what his opponent could see. As the great Atticus Finch says, 'sometimes, son, you need to wear the other guy's shoes.'

What is the Yugoslav seeing – what is his reality? For him, that bishop is no martyr but a kamikaze religious fanatic. Was he expecting it? He must have considered it. Has he seen the follow-up knight sacrifice? Probably, it's fairly obvious – it was just not obvious to me. Does he realise he's in the soup?

The bishop on h3 reminds me of that Ward-Suba game in the last round of the British Championships. Other players were strolling past their board and stopping to gawp, like visitors in an art gallery suddenly stunned into immobility by a beautiful canvas. I went to have a look myself, if only to get away from the car crash that I was involved in on my board. It was a conventional position from a Nimzo-Indian Defence: both sides castled, a few pieces out, time to move serenely into the middle game. Then Suba developed his queen's bishop, but instead of moving it to some normal square he long-leaped it all the way to the *verboten* square h3 where it could be taken by the dozing fianchettoed white bishop. For free. There was no attack, no ripping open the kingside, no immediate violence, no follow up. Just a black bishop sitting on h3 waiting to be taken. For nothing. I couldn't understand it. I'm not sure little Chris Ward understood it either. He was looking at that ghostly bishop haunting his position, trying to work out what was behind the visitation. Rubbing his hands together as if they were cold, although it was like a greenhouse in the playing hall, and chewing his lower lip. Meanwhile, Suba's puppet face was jolting up and down as he looked at the board, at Chris Ward, at the spectators, at me.

The rest of Eastbourne was oblivious to what was going on inside their Victorian theatre hall on that Friday afternoon; an Eastbourne subdued by the angry sun and the blowing up of their MP by the IRA the week before. Office workers were outside perspiring with their lunchtime sandwiches, the men with their jackets and ties off, the women with their skirt hems pulled up, shoes kicked off. The housewives were opening all the windows. Holiday-makers were shuffling along the front, carefully holding up their ice-creams, or collapsed in deck chairs with their tabloids. None of them knew that only a few hundred metres away, in that theatre hall – windows, doors, fire-escapes, skylights opened to let in the empty breeze – the best chess players of the second-best chess nation in the world were locked in a sweaty brawl for the final standings. A fight that combined Mike Tyson aggression with Steven Hawking brainpower and Picasso creativity. And that in their midst was an East European, allowed to play in the venerable British Championships, and, between cigarette breaks, he was crafting a work of art that people still unborn would appreciate years later.

The Yugoslav bends closer to that black bishop, his eyes inches away from its proud face, as if appreciating its corporeality will help him understand what to do with it. Of course, he knows he must execute it, even though it will lead to a violent uprising. Or could he be contemplating leaving the bishop alive? That can't be possible, surely? I'll just kamikaze it again on g2. Could Ward have declined Suba's bishop sacrifice? Let's see if I can recall that position… Suba had those big black pawns in the centre, and Ward had his queen on a4 of course, and Suba's queen was….

The Yugoslav lifts my bishop off his dying square, and replaces him with a glinting pawn. The bishop is laid to rest next to my queen's rook behind the clock. Another sacrifice to the great cause.

Chess time: White: 1 hour 12 minutes
Black: 1 hour 36 minutes

OK, there's no point pissing about here. You only sacrificed that bishop because you can follow up with the knight sacrifice. Although it feels counter-intuitive to give up that super-knight on f4. It was easier to give up the bishop that hadn't left his vestry all game, harder to give up a knight that is roaring in his prime. But the deed must be done and I throw the knight onto the blood-spattered h3 square.

And it feels good – I'm getting a high from sacrificing my pieces. This is what it's all about. That's why Tal keeps on playing even as his powers decline – chasing that sacrificer's high. Let us be sacrificers. But not butchers, like my opponent – ha ha.

He continues his trance on the h3 square as if the mysteries of life are hidden there. Other players walking past are noticing that Black is initiating a massive sacrificial attack, wondering at this English guy who has the courage and vision to play like this in the last round. Look at my works ye mighty. They walk on, relieved that it is the Yugoslav and not themselves on the receiving end of such violence. Come back Tal and have a look at my handiwork – I'm your real pupil, not that bequiffed Latvian on Board 1.

Dapper Andic is looking over at my position, assessing it in his clinical way. So, what do you think of that, my friend? You might have beaten me once but let me play you again and this is what I'll do to you. You won't be torturing me with a rook and bishop again, because you'll be dead a long time before that, ripped apart on the kingside. And then he looks up at me briefly before returning his gaze to his own board, but it's impossible to read what he might be thinking of my position or me.

I pretend to sniff, although I'm not sure why.

The Yugoslav replaces my knight on h3 with his bishop from the back row, and adds my knight to the necropolis of bodies behind the clock.

Chess time: White: 1 hour 14 minutes
Black: 1 hour 40 minutes
(Actually, some seconds less than the 40 minute mark, it's more like 1 hour 39 minutes.)

It took me half an hour to work that knight sacrifice out, it took him a minute to whip it off. The disparity between creation and destruction – hours to build a public telephone box, a minute to smash it up. It looks like he was expecting it. Why did it take *me* so long to see it?

Chess time: White: 1 hour 14 minutes
Black: 1 hour 39 minutes

There is only one move now to drive through my attack. With my queen. I need to work her into white's broken defences – her tall shadow will soon be darkening the white king. I write down the move, my hand quivering with adrenalin, and lean back to take a calm bird's eye view of the position. But I'm only looking at the plastic tops of the pieces, their outward form, not their inner realities. However, I've already done all that and know what needs to be done. I dink forward my dark queen, filled from head to toe with the direst cruelty.

I look around and there's Kolia, my Serbian friend, over by the entrance, come to see me. Shoulder-length black hair, black leather jacket, finally out of bed after last night. I wonder if he feels as rough as I did this morning. Probably not, he's probably inured to that *slivovitz* (for the first time the word itself doesn't launch a shock of nausea) – been drinking it since he was in his pram. And he's looking around, looking for me. But he looks uncertain – looks like he doesn't belong in here. Cool rocker in a library-like chess hall. Like when Lauren came to meet me at a blitz tournament in a school hall in London – this willowy blonde in a flowery dress and pink DMs standing out amid the geeky bespectacled kids and pasty middle-aged men bent over the school desks with their chessboards and clocks.

Kolia comes down the line of boards on my side. I lean back in my chair and smile at him, and sadly realise that this guy is younger, fresher faced, without the debauched look. And he's wearing basketball trainers – not cowboy boots like Kolia who's probably still sleeping after last night's session.

The Yugoslav's chin is resting on his chubby right hand, all his fingers in his mouth, looking like the village idiot… or a genius scientist…

This is *his* Critical Position. And he knows it. He must find a defence against the furnace-blast of my attack. But despite the weight of all his extra plastic, I can't see a good way for him. His king is cowering and shivering in the corner of the board, while his queen is miles away on the other side of the world. But what can he do? I don't know what he can do.

His cheeks are clamped between both fists, his knuckles lifting up the fat. His head is as heavy as bronze. He's searching the position, looking for a way to survive. His discomfort is boosting my confidence. But if there's one thing I've learnt, it's that confidence can be dangerous. Renshawe's Rule: When you're feeling confident, knuckle down and do some analysis.

So, I delve back into the position, back into the cake shop of variations. And all the goodies are still there on their shelves where I left them. I start to taste them again and they are all as delicious as last time. My mouth is watering at some of the possibilities. There is actual saliva in my mouth.

I have another look at the queen sacrifice variation – running through it like a memorised Larkin poem – each line working perfectly until the exquisite ending: the lone black knight delivering checkmate in front of the hopeless existence of the white war machine. Wow, that is good.

But hold on, I'm not analysing here, I'm just passively replaying variations that I've already worked out – as if fast forwarding on a video player. I'm not thinking. I need to challenge my variations. Look at the realities, rather than what I want to see. I need a coffee. No, I don't need a coffee. I need to do some work. Try to find a defence for him.

Head in hands I'm back in the shop, but this time I'm carefully reading the ingredients, checking the sell-by dates. And it all looks good until I see something he could play that I hadn't considered. A lunging rook sacrifice into my position that might disturb my communication. Surely, that's just nonsense? Although, I suppose it could gum up my attack for a bit, maybe buy him a couple of moves while I reorganise.

Hold on. A couple of moves is all he needs to arrange his defences. God, that could be a good move for him. Someone's put bleach in the cream puffs.

I look at ways to maintain my attack after giving him those two tempi, but it's all looking sluggish, my pieces lacking energy. As I search the position, my right leg is thumping like a piston. The empty coffee cups near my clock are vibrating. Animal looks across at my leg, drugged up eyes peering out from the haze of his long straggly hair. I glance at the slaughter-house of his position – come on, Animal, I'm not sure why you're worrying about me – that's a bit like someone with his head in the guillotine complaining about the clicks of the nearby knitting women. But I don't want to disturb my fellow combatants or alert my opponent to anything, so I clamp my leg with both hands and continue hunting the position after White's rook sacrifice.

But I can't re-energise my attack. I try to breathe another of Tal's spells into my pieces but the magic's gone. I try the moves of all my remaining pieces. To hell with candidate moves, I'm trying everything. When I'm checking whether moving my king would somehow kick-start the attack, I realise that I'm in the soup.

But will he see this counter-sacrifice? Probably. Especially as he's dead otherwise. Concentrates the mind wonderfully and all that. And a rook is small dinar to him at this stage. Jesus. How has it come to this? It was all looking so sweet. I feel like crying.

And he's shifting his hands away from his face, he's about to make his move, he's about to cruise-missile his rook into my pieces and end my dreams. What an idiot. Me or him? Both. I'm done in. It's ended. He pauses, his hand over the board. Hovering over my neck. Go on, do it, what are you waiting for? Finish me. But he doesn't make a move, instead he picks up his pen and stuffs it dummy-like in his mouth and continues studying the board.

And I look up at the high windows for I'm not sure what. To say a prayer to the sky. To say thanks for the stay of execution. For giving me a few more minutes of glorious life, during which I can continue hoping that he doesn't see the rook move. And the chess variations gradually clear from my head as I contemplate the darkening pewter sky, streaked through with scruffy black clouds – strangely beautiful and calming. And I realise that I don't even need to take his rook when he sacrifices it. I can just leave it sitting there in my position and it can't hurt me. Without even looking at the board I know that's the answer, and I suppress a silly grin and feel a sense of relief surging through me like a hot air balloon lifting off the ground.

Ah, that's good. A white rook deep in my position but I can just ignore it and press on with the onslaught. Just leave the rook where it is – advanced and impotent. That's so good, chess can be so good, life can be so good.

And now, with my heart thundering again, I'm hoping he *does* play the rook sacrifice. Has he seen it? Probably. But he probably saw immediately that it was nonsense.

But what can he play? How can he prevent his kingside from collapsing like a sandcastle before the tide of my attack?

It looks like he's eating his pen. I hope he doesn't swallow it. I don't want to leap over the board and perform the Heimlich manoeuvre on the guy. Have to save the Yugoslav's life – kill him on the board but save him in real life. Not that I know how to do the Heimlich manoeuvre.

Chess time: White: 1 hour 31 minutes
Black: 1 hour 40 minutes

Fantastic – he has time to worry about time now as well. He's heading towards 'time troubles', as the Continentals say. Although I guess he doesn't care – he's just trying to stay alive; if he can't stay alive then time becomes an irrelevance. Death stops time.

My hangover has officially ended and I'm feeling good about things – my mind is clear for the first time today, all my senses are engaged, reality sharpened. I relax for several breaths, one, two, three, enjoying the sensation of being alive.

I zone back onto the board. That white rook sacrifice looks like a prank move now – a rook covered in a white sheet with eye slits pretending to be a ghost. Can't believe it stopped my heart in terror. I have another look at the lovely queen sacrifice variation and feel even better. I can't stop looking at it. Please God, let that come to pass on the board. I can see a diagram of the final mating position in the *British Chess Magazine*, perhaps even on the front cover.

This might be a good time to go for another coffee. But I'm feeling thirsty so I might get a Coke instead. I'm feeling hungry as well – I've survived my hangover, and now I need to eat something. What time is it? Not chess time, but real time? I don't know and it doesn't really matter.

64 seconds with Sam Renshawe

Place of residence – London

Favourite food – Pie and mash with gravy

Favourite drink – Coffee, Coke, lager (if I've not had a bucket-full the night before)

Favourite sport – Football – not to play, just to watch

Favourite music – Pink Floyd

Favourite film – 'Withnail and I'

Favourite book – 'Ulysses' by James Joyce

Favourite Quotation – 'Education never ends, Watson. It is a series of lessons, with the greatest for last.'

Favourite chess book – 'Test of Time' by Kasparov. As a kid it was Fischer's 'My 60 Memorable Games'

Favourite chess player – Kasparov. As a kid it was Fischer

Best game – Mitrovic – Renshawe, Novi Sad Open, 1990 (the one with the famous queen sacrifice)

Best result – Second place, Novi Sad Open, 1990

The Yugoslav has started to sweat, small flecks on his forehead near his receding hairline, small islands forming under the armpits of his white shirt. He's chomping on his pen like it's a bone; fidgeting in his chair like a toddler who needs the toilet. The oceanic pressures of time and position crushing his tubby little body. And his discomfort is adding to my confidence – his pain is making me feel good. As Fischer said, 'I like to crush the other guy's ego.' But that's as much about himself as his opponent – using his opponent's decline to boost himself. The Yugoslav and I are like Richard II and Bolingbroke – *as his bucket-full of tears goes down into the depths of the well, mine raises up on high…* or something like that.

But at the same time, I feel sorry for the guy. I know what he's going through – only the chess player can truly understand the agonies suffered at the board. The empathy of the warrior for his adversary. I feel like reaching out and putting a calming hand on his shoulder and telling him that I know what he's feeling and that although he's lost he'll be OK, and invite him for a *pivo*. No, not sure I'll be ready for another *pivo*. Maybe, I'll offer him a coffee instead. Anyway, let's wait for the game to finish first.

On my right, a shell-shocked Animal offers his hand in resignation to the Tooth-Fairy. He's about to lose his queen or get mated or both. Poor guy never got out the opening. Years of chess training, hours spent on opening preparation, tense moments psyching yourself up before the game, and you get ripped apart before your pieces come off the first rank. And by someone who looks like the Tooth-Fairy. Sorry Animal, that's just the way it goes sometimes. The players don't say anything as they exchange scoresheets for signing. The old chief arbiter – in his navy three piece suit like a British Rail conductor – sidles up to take the scoresheets. He leans over and stops their clock, calmly lying his whole pale hand over both buttons to silence it.

The two players are up on their feet, the Tooth-Fairy seems to be looking around for someone or something, his eyes blinking; Animal is folding his scoresheet into his pocket, collecting his pen from the table, looking at, but not seeing, my position. Adjusting to the bracing change from chess time to real time. It can take a while to recover. When I came back from the British Championship qualifier on that Sunday night, Lauren wanted to meet up but I told her I needed to rest because I felt a bit jet-lagged. '*Jet-lagged*? You've just come back from Brighton.'

The Tooth-Fairy and Animal wander off and the right-hand house in our terrace has gone. I now have a clear view across to Board 5. I move my tower of coffee cups over to Animal's table, enjoying my additional *Luft*.

The Yugoslav, head burrowed in his sweaty hands, is not aware that we've lost our neighbours. He's one with the chessboard, locked in chess time.

Chess time: White: 1 hour 39 minutes
Black: 1 hour 40 minutes

And he's only got about twenty minutes of that left. One of his spasms knocks his grey cardigan/coat off the back of his chair. It sprawls onto the floor behind his chair and lies there like a dead cat. He doesn't even notice. Should I tell him? No, never disturb a man when he's thinking about his position, especially not when he's in the soup. But it's a good omen for me.

Maybe I should go next door and check on the England match? And see how the US are doing against Bulgaria? Do I have time? He's going to have to make his move soon and I don't want my clock to start running down. But I want to see how Murray and John are doing. I'm sure they'll only need one win and a draw for silver, maybe not even that – and if anyone can do it, Murray and John can. Especially against Cuban amateurs. It's going to be a good day for Sammy and England. And St. George – ha ha. But I'm not sure I've time. I'm going to need some thinking time for the final push. I've probably got time to get a Coke though. And a Mars Bar. Sustenance to see me through the denouement, the final chapter...

But hold on, I should be analysing, checking variations, finding a defence for him. 98% concentration even during his time. I look again at that White rook sacrifice possibility that nearly gave me a heart attack and it looks ridiculous. I look at my queen sacrifice variation again. That's good. That variation is lovely and visual, like a Nabokov sentence. I want to show that to someone. I should go and get a Coke to celebrate…

But what's going on next door on my left? Andic and the German kid are leaning over their board, foreheads nearly touching, whispering to each other. What's going on? What are they chatting about in the middle of the game? Hey, no talking over there, you'll disturb my opponent. The knobs on their clocks are both at half-mast, chess time has ended there as well. They've agreed a draw. OK, so they've both decided to take the prize money that they're guaranteed for half a point, rather than risk the chance of zilch for a loss. Good for me as I will overtake them both. But surprising. It was the start of Act 4, the crisis point just reached, the plot rich in possible developments, and now they'll never know the ending. The chief arbiter arrives at their table to clear the stage. Andic and the German kid leave together for the analysis room – to convince each other how it would've ended. Then Andic will quiz the kid about the political situation in Germany. Will there be enough jobs for those in the East? If not, will they find work in the West? How many East Germans have already piled through the wall?

And should I go through the wall? Go and find Lauren? Call Kolia and tell him that I want to go with him to Berlin? No, that was all drunken nonsense. The guy was pissed, and I was even more pissed. Even if I found her, what would she say if I turned up at her university in Berlin? I'm sure she's moved on. Found a non-chess player, someone more normal as she deserves. It's probably time for me to move on as well. I remember all the good times with her but I forget all the frustrations as well – the times when she didn't want me to play chess. She always seemed slightly reluctant to share in my victories; she even seemed resentful of my qualification to the British Championships. And the chess is going well – I'm going to come second here. And then who knows? I need to get better and I'm going to need all my time to focus on it. No, I'm not Romeo nor was I meant to be – I'm a chess player. Let's win this game and go home.

As the arbiter dodders off – his glasses, on a string around his neck, resting on his waistcoated paunch – he notices the Yugoslav's coat/cardigan on the floor. He stoops down arthritically to pick it up and gently replaces it on the back of his chair. The Yugoslav is oblivious to it. He's like the sleeping kid unaware that his dad is rearranging his blanket while he's dreaming. Or having a nightmare.

So, that's both sets of neighbours moved out. The Yugoslav and I are on our own. I don't have to worry about Andic's stare anymore, nearly as bad as when I was sitting opposite him. I can see clearly across to Board 1 – the young Latvian, Tal's protégé, with his blond quiff, glaring balefully at his opponent. This evening he'll show his game to Tal in his hotel room – telling him the story of his game, recounting all the variations he calculated. And Tal will nod along with him, cigarette ablaze in one hand, glass of whisky glowing in the other. Then Tal will lean forward, motion with his sloshing glass for his pupil to stop, and he'll direct him to the possibility of a fiendish knight sacrifice. And it'll be Tal's turn to whipcrack though variations, to start creating, making art, and as he does he'll forget Latvia's Olympiad ban and his respiratory problems and his one kidney, and he'll be in his early twenties again, crunching Fischer in a vortex of tactics in Belgrade.

I'm going to go and have a look at the Latvian's position. No, stay here, don't get distracted – the Yugoslav is going to make a move soon and I'm going to need to finish him off. It seems as if he's looking over at my queenside. God knows why. There's nothing more going on there. My queenside is razed to the ground, even the smouldering smoke has gone out – your queen has taken everything, you can do no more damage there, my friend. He should be looking at the kingside, trying to cover up his king who's out there on the heath with his gonads exposed.

Yes, I'm going to become more serious about my chess. Start training properly. I'm going to study endgames. Work my way through Averbakh's endgame books, systematically, analysing hard like Speelman, testing myself, making notes. I'm going to cut down on the booze as well, and the junk food, and do some exercise, some running. I'm going to get good at this game and go back to the British Championships next year and land some punches of my own.

The Yugoslav removes his right hand from his cheek and floats it over the board. He's finally going to make a move. It hovers there like one of those claw cranes in the arcades above the little toys. Which furry piece is he going to pick up? But no, the wavering hand retracts to his cheek.

That's it, I'm getting a coke.

13

Out in the corridor the cold air from outside is sneaking in though the external doors. And there in front of the coffee table is the tumbling dark hair of Alisa Maric in tight high jeans, purple mohair jumper and the same shiny black shoes she was wearing at the Lloyds Bank Masters in the summer. Jessica Rabbit figure. Very different to Lauren's tall delicate angularity. She is saying something in Serbo-Croatian to the frizzy-haired student behind the table. I queue next to her but keep a distance, reluctant to enter her dizzying forcefield. She has high cheekbones and a mouth sculpted into a red pout, rendered even more beautiful by that mole above her lips – a Nabokovian touch of genius. The fantasy girlfriend of every chess player…

But what would the reality be like? What would it really be like to have a much stronger player, a chess celebrity, as your girlfriend? Sharing her with chess – you'd be the one staying at home waiting for her return from dazzling spectators and players at international tournaments. And what would she think of your own chess pretensions? She'd soon be dismissing your move suggestions with a frown, preferring to wash her superb hair than look at your games, refusing to play you at blitz because you're an idiot. She would be no Miranda happy for you to beat her by cheating…

No Sam, she's just a fantasy. The reality was Lauren…

'What is that God-awful smell?' she asked, theatrically holding her nose, as we walked down the brutalist concrete corridor of my tower block.

'Welcome to Victory Mansions. That's my East German neighbour who has a penchant for cooking cabbages. He's supposed to be a defector who went on the run in the seventies.'

'That's horrible. Well, maybe he'll be able to return soon, and he'll take his *penchant* and cabbages with him,' she said, still clothes-pegging her nose. Her fine small nose.

'Well, here we are, this door leads to chez Renshawe.'

'Well, get the door open quickly. Dat smell is doo much.'

I fumbled in my damp leather jacket for my keys. Despite the beer I'd drunk, I could still feel the glow of tension in my stomach. Lauren's physical presence, her reality in front of me was making me woozily nervous – her hay-coloured fringe glistening with rain, her eyes shining with cider fizz behind the lenses of her big glasses, her heart-stopping smile, her bulky green Parka that reached down to her knees like a dress, her bare shins still summer brown in September, and her chunky black DMs emphasising the fragility of those legs.

Since our first meeting in the University Main Library we'd gone for tea and cake a couple of times and I'd joined her and her friends for a pub quiz. But this was our first 'date'. In the afternoon, we'd visited a Turner exhibition at the Tate Gallery, pissing about among the pensioners and school groups, then we'd returned to Great Portland Street station, dashing across the rain to the Green Man for a 'post-exhibition discussion'. She was drinking halves of Strongbow to my pints of Carling. Once I'd had enough beer to soft-focus reality, I'd idly suggested that she could come with me 'to see my flatlet'.

I'd been calculating ways to kiss her all day, spending far more time looking at her face than the Turners, but talking myself out of forcing the critical moment. Her mouth just too beautiful for one of my kisses. And what if she said that wasn't what she wanted? After the pub, I'd grabbed her hand as we avoided the cars swishing through the rain on Euston Road but she'd let go on the other side – or had I?

I dropped my keys on the concrete corridor floor and scrambled to pick them up, giving me a close-up of her DMs, her smooth shins, her parka, and finally her pouting lips, and without thinking I ducked under the hand holding her nose, into the flood of clean citrusy perfume, and gave her a salty rain-tasting kiss.

'Thank God that's ended,' she said once we were inside the flat.

'I hope you mean the smell and not the kiss?'

'Both,' she said. She looked at me. 'Don't worry Sam, I'm only joking,' and she lightly touched my hair, her perfume drowning my senses. I was relieved she didn't come any closer because of the immense erection that was straining against my jeans. But at the same time, I wanted to grab her and start kissing her again, to put my hands all over her, but her reality was too much – her thin body concealed in that big parka, her cool clean skin. Who was I to disturb all that? And that wry smile looking at me, telling me that was not what she wanted.

'Wow, your own flat – you're so lucky. I'd so much love to

move out of halls. You're the only student I know who has their own flat. Soooo, are you going to give me the tour?'

'Well, there's not much to see really – you can see it all from here. It's more like a box than a flat. There's only three rooms. Here on the left is the bathroom.' With its memory of that morning's long blast of cherry air freshener.

'Your own bath. You know, that's something I really miss in halls – they only have these stinky old showers. I love taking baths, you know just sinking down and relaxing in the water, reading a paperback.' And the thought of her long brown naked body – shed of Parka, dress, DMs – outstretched in my bath, gave my erection such force that I giddily gripped the door jamb. I wanted to say, 'You can have one here if you want,' but instead said, 'Yes, me too, baths can be very nice. And this is the living room, as you can see.' I stretched out my arm to the thin room – worn settee in front of a book-covered coffee table, hire-purchase television, MFI self-assembly bookshelf – which ended in a recessed plastic kitchenette and a window that looked out onto the concrete wall of another tower block, most of its windows lit up.

'You see, it's not much is it?'

'Yes, but it's your own space… it's a room of your own,' she said in a Virginia Woolf voice.

'Yes, true, it's a good place to concentrate when I'm not in the library. D'you want something to drink? I haven't got any cider but I think I might have some cheap white wine in the fridge.'

'I don't think I could drink any more cider to be honest, but I love cheap white wine.'

I went into the kitchenette, relieved to be away from her immediate perfumed presence. I needed some time for my heartbeat to reduce. She went to the bookshelf bending forward to look at the framed photo of my dad and me. I'm pale and morose, looking away at something in the distance, while my dad, already shorter than me, is soppy-stern, squinting towards the camera.

'That was taken in our last summer together in Margate, you know, before. We used to go every summer. Have you ever been there, to Margate?'

'No, I haven't. My parents didn't want to spend time on crowded British beaches, so we spent time on crowded French ones instead.'

'You don't know what you've been missing. Margate's great. Maybe we could go there together.'

She looked at me.

'For a day trip, I mean.'

'Yes, maybe we could.' She looked at the photograph again. 'He looks just like you, it's you but without the hair.'

'Yes, I've got that to look forward to.'

'My friend Alex, who's already started to lose his hair, and he's only twenty-two or something, told me that genetically you get baldness from your mother's side, so your mother's father, not your own.'

'Well, my granddad was as bald as a coot as well, so I've got no hope.'

She peered at the spines of books on my bookshelf, slowly running her finger over their tops as if checking for dust.

'You've got loads of books on James Joyce.'

'Yep… I sort of collect books on Joyce.' I nearly told her that I'd read Ellman's biography about twenty times but didn't want her thinking I was an obsessive weirdo.

'Ah, this is the one you were reading when I first saw you in the library?'

'Yep.'

'You were so engrossed in that book – you looked like a lost little boy.'

'Did I?'

'Yes, you did.' And she looked at me, biting her lower lip, sexily, as if she were thinking about something else. As if she knew something that I didn't, and never would.

'Are you learning Spanish?'

'No, not that I know of. English is hard enough for me.'

'Well, you've got a book here, 'Mastering Spanish'.'

She'd got to the end of the shelf where I kept a few chess books, a handful from the hundreds I had boxed up at my mum's. 'That's not 'Mastering Spanish', but 'Mastering *the* Spanish'. It's a chess book. The Spanish is a way of opening the game.'

'What, a whole book on a way of starting a game?'

'Yep, and there are books on sub-variations in the Spanish Opening, and then even books on sub-sub-variations. Whole books. It's vastly complicated.'

'*Play the Dutch-Leningrad*, she read out. 'What's the connection between Holland and Leningrad?'

'I don't know, but it's another name for an opening defence.'

'And what's this one? *Beating the Sicilian*. What did the Sicilian ever do?'

'Yeh, I suppose that does sound strange, but the Sicilian is the name for another defence and that book teaches you how to play against it.'

'How to beat it?'

'That's the one.'

'You didn't tell me you played chess. You didn't tell me you were a secret chess geek.'

'I don't really. I mean I look at it sometimes, and maybe solve a puzzle or two in the bath or on the train or something, but I don't play anymore. I used to play a lot when I was a kid – in competitions and things. To be honest, for a time I was completely addicted. But I gave it up. I suppose I stopped playing properly when I came to university.'

'Why did you give it up?'

'Not sure really. I suppose it was taking up too much of my time. And I wasn't really getting anywhere with it. I was putting in a lot of effort for not much reward. And around that time, I was getting interested in other things… I wanted to concentrate on other things…'

'What, like taking women to pubs and plying them with strong cider?'

'Yeah, that sort of thing.' I smile. 'Followed by plying them with cheap wine.'

I handed her a glass of Sainsbury's wine, moving back into her aura of unnerving reality.

'And do you miss it? Playing chess?'

I take a sip of the acidic wine, thinking about the exhilaration of leading a sacrificial mating attack, the insomnia-inducing low of an avoidable defeat, the hours of solitary study, head in hands, staring into the abysmal depths of chess. 'Yes, as ex-smokers say, you always miss it. I keep thinking about playing a bit again. A few games for the university or something. But I've got a very addictive personality – when I get started on something I can end up doing it to the exclusion of everything else. And then I stop going out and stop talking to people. So,

I sort of actively try to avoid it. And, I've got my research to do...' I waved to the coffee table covered with multi-coloured Arden edition Shakespeares.

'Ah I see... that's where you find your 'striking juxtapositions' is it?'

'Very funny, yes, I fill my notebooks with them. I've got loads more for you when you're ready... But maybe I'll get back to the chess after I've finished my PHD.' I glugged more of the wine and said, 'But I would much rather spend time with you than be playing chess.'

'Wow, Sam, that's one of the most romantic things anyone's ever said to me.' She gave me her half-cocked smile then sipped her wine and screwed her face up like a little girl taking her medicine. 'Wow, that is cheap.' She giggled. 'And that door on the left – that you've not shown me – I'm assuming that's your bedroom?'

'Yes.' Lauren in my bedroom. Jesus. 'Do you want to have a look at that as well?'

'Why not?'

I opened the door. 'Voila!' I was proud of the bedroom; it had a modern feel to it compared to the seventies décor of the rest of the flat – hanging rails for my clothes rather than a wardrobe, faux-wooden lino instead of shaggy carpet, clean whitewashed walls instead of the stewed tea wallpaper, and one of those white duvets on the bed instead of sheets and blankets. Lauren in my bed. Naked. Sweet Jesus. The room was pumping with blood. Should I just kiss her again and push her onto the bed? Did she want that? Instead I said, 'And this is the bedroom.'

'Yes, I can see that.' Then she said, unsmilingly, 'but you do know that I won't be going in there, don't you, Sam?'

'No, no, of course not. I mean yes, of course. No, I didn't think you would. I mean I just thought you wanted to see it.'

She smiled at me again. Then she took my hand, tugging me towards the living room, and leaned so close to my ear that I could feel the heat of her cider breath as she whispered clearly, slowly, 'We won't be going in there, because I want to start on the sofa.'

The following morning, after Lauren had left early for the library, softly clicking the bedroom door then the flat door, I wallowed under the duvet for a long time with a luxurious hangover, in an in-between world, a *Zwischenzug*, of sleep and wakefulness, dreams and reality, remembering the night before, trying to recreate it, to relive it, to improve it. Trying to control it. Wondering how I'd rolled the universe into a ball.

When I finally got up I sent Lauren the post card that I'd bought at the Tate Gallery. On the front was Turner's 'Sunrise'. On the back I wrote:

My lovely Lauren,
I'd like to be your only audience,
The final name in your appointment book,
Your future tense.
All my love,
Sam

Slowly, without looking back, Alisa Maric goes down the corridor back to her chess time in the Olympiad playing hall. I return to my playing hall with a cool bottle of Coke and a Mars Bar.

I sit down carefully so as not to disturb my opponent who's rocking back and forth, his arms wrapped around his chest as if he's wearing a strait jacket. Body twisted out of shape. His mouth gurning, little tremors like worms around his flabby jaw.

Chess time: White: 1 hour 50/51 minutes
*   Black: 1 hour 40 minutes*

He's got under ten minutes remaining. Is he just going to sit there going mad until he runs out of time? Wait until they carry him out on a strapped stretcher?

I take a drag of Coke. Ah, that's good – the syrupy cold liquid washing out my mouth. I look at the solid Mars Bar lying on the shiny wooden table. The red and black packet reminding me of the cover of Kasparov's *Test of Time*. I pick it up and am surprised and satisfied at how heavy it is, like a weighted chess piece. I'm about to unpeel the wrapper when my opponent extricates himself from his self-hug, leans heavily over to my queenside, and shifts his queen one square. He restarts my clock.

14

What the hell is that?

I put the unopened Mars Bar back on the table. That's not a move. You can't be moving your queen over there, son. That's not going to help you. Why are you making an irrelevant move at the furthest point from where the action is? Have you given up? Have you gone mad?

I can just take all his pieces on the kingside like Pac-Man – chomp, chomp, chomp – and checkmate his lone king.

It was his Critical Moment when he had to find a defensive move and he moves his queen, who's miles away on the queenside, effectively on another board – she's making no threats, there's no point. He spent fifty minutes, a bucket-full of sweat, and his sanity for that. I restrain myself from shaking my head, from laughing, from calling over the arbiter and telling him that my opponent's not fit to continue.

I scribble the joke move down and my hand is calm for the first time since the opening – Qb7 – it even looks stupid on paper. For the first time, I know with certainty – with both head and stomach – that I will win this game. That everything has worked out, that all the sacrifices were the right ones, that everything has connected. And that all the sacrifices in the months leading up to this game were also worth it. All those hours invested in my pocket set, including the wasted ones, the time spent away from my PHD. Time spent away from Lauren. Even the rupture with Lauren as painful as that was. It was all necessary to be here at this moment in time defeating a Yugoslav master and taking second place in this tournament. And it feels good.

I've nothing to think about here. If he's going to let me mow his kingside like grass then I'm going to do it. Nothing's going to stop me. It's time to cash in.

My vampiric queen, aching for blood, begins her carnage. I take his rook off the board, enjoying the feel of its crenellations under my index finger and place it on the table carefully next to my Mars Bar. A big fat rook. The first of my plunder. I'm going to be rich.

For the first time in the game I didn't write down my move before playing it and conduct a blunder check. The Blumenfeld Rule. It's usually a bad sign when I forget that. But here it really doesn't matter – I'm Pac-Man munching through his kingside, and the ghosts are very far away.

The Yugoslav looks like a pounded slab of meat, slumped back in his chair. He's sweating like a tennis player, eyes blinking arrhythmically, fingers twitching over his beer belly. I'm sure he wants to be a long way from here – back in his armchair in his slippers at home (wherever that is) with his family (if he has one), far away from all this ultraviolence.

He straightens up, uses both hands to pull his sticky shirt away from his body, and bends forward, putting his face close to the clock – as if he were looking at it through a magnifying glass – to gauge exactly where the minute hand is, to understand precisely how much chess life he has left.

Chess time: White: 1 hour 54 minutes
Black: 1 hour 40 minutes

Not much, I can tell you – about five minutes for another ten moves. He's like Marlowe's Faust at the end, waiting for the devil to come and drag him down to hell at midnight, and praying for time to stop. But he knows that time must run and the clock must strike, and that the end is coming and there's nothing he can do about it.

He jerkily reaches his hand out. Is that it, is he calling it a day, is he resigning? No, he's moving his queen again – one doddery step back again.

What's he doing? Is he just going to let me take everything on the kingside? Give everyone up to the slaughter of my queen? He's not even making a token effort at protecting himself over there. He has no threats, no plans, no prospects.

Time for my Mars Bar. I pick up the chunky bar again running my hand over its pleasing ridges beneath the dark wrapper.

Well… not exactly *no* prospects I suppose – he's retreating his queen, that's what he's doing, he's extricating her from the queenside. Pulling her out. But surely he can see that's too slow, that the evacuation takes too many moves? While he's doing that I'll eat all his pieces and finish off with king pie. His estranged queen is too rheumatic to be on time. She simply doesn't have enough time…

OK, but I better check that. I put the Mars Bar back on the table next to the bloated corpse of the white rook.

OK… I'm right to spend some time here because he does have a way to wend his queen back to the kingside. And he is just in time to stop me from checkmating him. Amazingly, his queen will arrive in the bedchamber just as my queen is about to put the axe to his king. Is there a literary equivalent for that? A queen protecting her king from the deadly advances of another queen. In Shakespeare? Can't think of any. In Greek tragedy? Not sure... anyway, let's not worry about that now. Need to clarify what's going on here when that white queen arrives...

OK... so she can exchange herself off for my queen. To save her husband. But so what? He'll stop the checkmate, but by then I'll have wiped out his whole army. Every queen move costs him a piece. I'll recover all my sacrificed plastic with hefty interest. And swiftly knock him out in the endgame with my extra material. No problemo, Manuel.

But how much extra material will I have in that endgame? I better check that as well...

OK... so I'll be at least a pawn up, probably two. That'll easily be enough. I would've preferred to have ended it with that beautiful queen sacrifice but that's chess. A win's a win.

I move my queen, hacking off one of his knights. The Yugoslav peers at the clock, glances at his disappearing kingside, looks at the clock again, and lopes his queen back to the corner of his queenside.

So that was his idea, that was what he found during his mammoth think – sacrifice everything on the kingside to buy time to bring back his queen, bounce her all the way round the board like a snooker ball, to assist her king. It's a clever idea, I'll give him that. But I guess it was the only way to stay on the board, the only way to somehow reach an endgame. Even if it's hopeless.

My queen crunches his other knight. His queen continues her rescue plan. The main feast is over but it's time for the After Eights. My queen gobbles one of his pawns. His queen shifts onto its final stretch. My queen slips down another pawn and is burping in the white king's bedroom when his wife bursts in. A female Odysseus. Just in time, my friend. It is barely believable that his queen has journeyed all the way back from my queenside corner square. It looked physically impossible, mathematically impossible. It's aesthetically very pleasing. It's almost sad that it doesn't save him.

We exchange our fatigued queens. I'm sorry to see mine leave the board – she deserved to finish him off. She should have died hereafter.

OK, it's time to take stock. I grab the Coke bottle, its glass cooling my clammy palm.

So, my attack has dried up, but his pieces are contorted horribly, I'm a solid pawn up, and he's got about three minutes left for six moves. I thought I might be able to nab another of his pawns but it looks like he can hold on to it. But no worries, one extra will be enough.

Glug of reassuring Coke. So how to proceed? How to realise my advantage? I need to adjust psychologically. I've been in hurly-burly attack mode for most of the game, it's time to change into sober endgame mode.

OK, so first I need to rearrange my pieces. As always, after a concentrated assault on one wing they have become a tad uncoordinated. It shouldn't be too difficult – just follow Capablanca's advice: imagine where I want them, and put them there...

It'll require a bit of shuffling about, some retreating before advancing, but it shouldn't be too tricky to organise. I take up the Mars Bar again and tear open the wrapper unleashing its dark caramel smell.

But hold on… how do I reactivate my pieces? How do I get them where I want them? I need to stop looking at this like Capablanca and do some analysis. Look at this properly… some gritty calculation to find the truth, rather than airy-fairy, Mars Bar-eating generalities. I put the Mars Bar back on the table and clamp my head in my hands…

Maybe this endgame is not as winning for me as I thought, even though I'm a pawn up. I need to energise my pieces but how? His rocky pawn promontory is still jutting deep into the centre of my position, cutting the links between my kingside and queenside. How to move my pieces? I haven't got very much space, I haven't got any air to breathe. I can't breathe…

A nameless dread starts to swirl in my stomach and oozes out to take over my whole body.

You've been looking at an illusion, at shadows on the wall of the cave. He's going to awaken his pieces and send them stomping into your position. And you're not going to be able to stop him because your pieces have no space. He'll steal back his pawn and another and another then help himself to your wallet.

I can't believe this. After the brilliant star-burst of the middlegame, without realising it, I'm left on the arid planet of a dead endgame: a black bishop blocked in by his own pawns and no space. The congenital and deadly disease of the King's Indian. The King's Indian is all beauty and vitality in youth, but it already carries the virus that will kill it in old age. That's why you've got to strike in the middle-game because by the endgame your position will be pock-marked by sickness. And that's what you're looking at now...

How did this happen? I'm like John Self in *Money* who, at the end of his climactic chess match with Martin Amis, reaches the *trebuchet* position and with sighs of relief thinks it's a draw, not realising he's in deadly *zugzwang*. But I'm worse than John Self because he was ignorant about the *trebuchet* position, whereas I know all about the King's Indian bad endgame. I've read all the books, gained all the knowledge, but I've still let it happen. I've ended up in a chess cliché. I am a cliché. You've got all the know-what but none of the know-how. All the knowledge but no wisdom. What a loser.

And does my opponent know how good this is for him? Probably... he's no idiot, he's a Yugoslav master, although he still looks stressed – underarm sweat patches like Greenland, Bugs Bunny gnawing of his pen, his eyes flitting from board to clock, from clock to board. He's been under pressure for so long that he might be thinking with his emotions, rather than his head, unable to see the truth. Although even if he doesn't realise it now, he soon will. After the Move Forty Time Control, he'll know...

So, maybe I should offer a draw? Catch him now while he doesn't know what's going on. After all, I'm a pawn up. It'll alert him to the fact that I'm not confident about my position anymore but it doesn't matter. If we keep playing I'm dead.

I retreat my offside rook, look confidently at my opponent's rabbitty face and say loudly, 'Draw'. Not as a question but as a statement. It's the first word I've said to this guy who's been sitting a couple of feet opposite me for nearly four hours.

The first thing he does is look at his clock. That's a good sign – he's seeing how long he has left (about three minutes) – he has a decision to make.

He takes the carrot out of his mouth and peers into the crystal ball of the board. What is he seeing? Hopefully, zilch.

He stops his fidgeting. He stops moving at all, bowing in front of the board as if at prayer. I can see the incipient bald patch on his crown. Less than three minutes left.

And I've stopped moving as well, my heart beats filling up the hushed hall while I await his verdict. Please let me off.

The minute hand of his clock has hoisted his blood-red flag to almost horizontal. About two minutes away from falling, probably less. He's not even looking at his clock anymore – is he just going to let his flag fall and lose on time?

This tension is too much. I need the toilet again.

He must have about a minute left – he's going to accept.

I stop breathing.

He looks at his clock. Shakes his head like he's just received a blow. Moves one of his pieces forward, slams his clock and says, 'I play,' sounding like a James Bond villain.

I exhale. He knows.

He only has a minute left for five moves. But they're easy moves. He just brings his pieces out, develops them like a second opening. His aged position recapturing its lost youth. While mine is dying. I can't make any threats. All I can do is scramble around with my pieces trying breach the gaps, but there are too many. I've got no space. And no position.

He maintains his monkish posture, oblivious to everything except board and clock, clock and board. He moves his piece and slashes his hand over to his clock in robotic fast-forward.

Like a trickster moving the cards around on the top of a cardboard box. He's done this before. He's not going to lose on time.

I'm not calculating now, not thinking about anything really except how bad this is going to look once we reach Move Forty. Will I be on life support or will the machine already be turned off?

The old chief arbiter is lurking behind my opponent with clipboard and pen, his steel-rimmed glasses on his face.

The Yugoslav makes his fortieth move – a huge bishop leap – and his hand darts out like a frog's tongue, slapping the top of his clock with his palm, almost knocking it over. It judders on the table while he collapses back into his chair, exhaling all the stress of the last few moves, of the last four hours, like he's just crossed the line at the end of a marathon, although one in which he's beaten his personal best.

Once I've made my fortieth move – moving my knight which is all dressed up with nowhere to go – the arbiter leans in and checks that everything is in order. I'm moved by his fatherly concern and it saddens me to know that the next time he comes it will be to collect our scoresheets and my body. Do we need to wind the clocks back? No, we just let them run. Another hour each for the next twenty moves. Not that this game is going to last another twenty moves.

It's my opponent's move and we're starting again – coming out for the second half, and I'm a couple of goals down and my goalkeeper's been sent off. I notice my uneaten Mars Bar laying like a turd next to the clock. I'm not hungry any more. I feel sick. I need a walk. I hope England are doing better than me…

15

The Olympiad playing hall is thrumming with the Time Control, pockets of musketry as players blitz it out to Move Forty – their country's fortunes decided by split-second decisions in cosmically complicated positions. Tremulous draw offers, relieved acceptances, stony refusals, death-faced resignations. Players signing and exchanging score-sheets, priest-like arbiters stopping clocks and resetting pieces. Spectators pool around the blitz exchanges, as if they were cock-fights, relishing the high-speed violence and unpredictability. I pass an African in a blue bobble hat who clatters over most of the pieces in his desperation to make a move, his eyes wide in fear. An Einstein-haired arbiter rushes over as to a toddler who's fallen on his face.

The student helpers in their black cocktail dresses swish around with renewed purpose. I pass one of them – tall, straight-backed – monitoring the Yugoslavia-China match, walking on the balls of her feet, tightening her delicate black-stockinged calves, to avoid her high-heels clicking on the floor.

A football crowd is jostling in front of the top boards. The odd cough or whisper but none of the shouting and whistling that accompanied every move of Fischer's near miss against Tal in Belgrade. Game 17. I look up at the giant demonstration boards – state-of-the-art electronic, not the wooden boards on easels that little kids were operating at the British Championships and Lloyds Bank Masters during the summer. The white pieces on the demonstration boards are ghostly pale under the hall's ceiling lights.

Murray's only gone and won again. I knew he'd do it. Well done, son. That guy's the Gary Lineker of chess. Nunn has reached Move Forty but he's badly in the soup. Exchange down. His position looks worse than mine. He's not going to survive that. 2-2 against Cuba. Hope that's enough. It means the Americans need three and a half against the Bulgarians to take clear second. Could they do it? How are they doing?

Seirawan and Benjamin both drew; DeFirmian chalked the full point; and Federowicz is still playing. So, they can't overtake us, but they could draw level if Federowicz wins, then it's down to tiebreak. Which could be bad news for England.

Federowicz has everything I want: a good endgame with Black. Exchange up. On tip-toe, peering over the wigs of the spectators, I see Federowicz at the board, his face obscured by his pop-star hair, his head resting on his boxer's fists – 98% concentration. He's going to win that endgame. No doubt about it. So it'll be down to tie-break. I think England might have blown it.

Nigel Short is standing within the fenced-off playing area, looking at Nunn's position, holding his chin with his right hand, head slightly cocked. He has a red and white scarf around his neck, and looks like a school prefect, although he's a few years older than me. Like Fischer and Polgar, he was a cruncher of grandmasters when he was a kid. Will he ever become world champion though? Done in by Speelman in the

Candidates last time, he's back in thanks to his superhuman last round win against Gurevich in Manilla. But so are the young guns – Gelfand and Ivanchuk – and they look hungrier, more equipped, more lethal. And even if he gets through them, myriad-minded Kasparov will be waiting patiently, licking his lips in front of the cave where he keeps his crown. The crown which he'll surely keep after that gritty endgame win at the weekend in France. Is it already too late for Short? Does he already know?

All dreaming sportsmen have that juddering moment of self-awareness when they know they're not going to make it. The young footballer who realises that he'll never play for England, the tennis player who realises he'll never play at Wimbledon. And every chess player has his moment when he knows that he'll never become world champion.

Mine came reasonably early, or probably late, in France, thanks to a former world champion. It was the summer holidays before I was to start Sixth Form and I'd responded to an ad at the back of *Chess* about a simultaneous display to be given by Boris Spassky in Brittany, securing a place by writing to the President of Dinard Chess Club, Monsieur Gilbert de Morgan, in my best O-level French. I used the prize money from winning a London junior tournament and two twenties handed over by my dad – *Is that any good to you, son?* – and took the ferry from Portsmouth to St Malo. I had a bag with a toothbrush and a comb in, and Fischer's *My 60 Memorable Games*, and spent the crossing breathing in his inspiration. What better way to prepare for Spassky than studying his vanquisher? But I also made sure I played through Game 18 again – Spassky's demolition of Fischer – to see what you should not do.

Sixteen of us (all French apart from me) formed a large square behind our boards on white clothed tables in the faded ballroom of a sea-side hotel. There were muted words of French – encouragements and jocularities – as we awaited Spassky's arrival. I was breathing through my nose to calm my nerves before the encounter, imagining I was Fischer in Reykjavik.

This short elderly gent came into the room whom I first took to be one of the organisers. I had been waiting for the Spassky of 1972. This guy looked like an affable history teacher – thick grey hair above a pleasant, slightly rubbery face, sensible old person's shoes, khaki trousers, cheap brown blazer. This guy has no chance against me, I thought, maybe the Spassky that played Fischer, but not this geriatric.

I shut out the world and poured myself into the game – neither before nor since have I worked so hard during a game, or at anything. Only once did I leave the board, when I jogged to and from the toilet. It was the defining moment of my life so far. To beat Spassky and emulate Fischer in Reykjavik, to become Fischer.

I sacrificed a pawn on the black side of a Sicilian Najdorf, winning the initiative and ludicrous complications, but Spassky steered through the turmoil and emerged unscathed into an endgame with his extra pawn, which he relentlessly converted with clean, machine-like chops. When I resigned, he shook my hand, said, 'Oui', and moved on to the next board.

He won every game except two. And those were two short draws that he chivalrously gave to the only two female participants. I doubt Fischer would have done the same.

At the end of the event he sat at a table meeting the players and signing their score sheets. Someone had provided him with a bulbous glass of red wine. While I waited in the queue, clutching Fischer's *My 60 Memorable Games*, I rehearsed all the questions I was going to ask him about our game. But when it came to my turn he didn't seem to recognise me. He shook my hand, and said, 'Enchanté de vous rencontrer'. I was hoping for some sort of blessing – 'You play like the young Fischer,' or 'You have a great chess future ahead of you, young man,' or even 'That was a very interesting pawn sacrifice,' but instead he said, to the amusement of the hovering Monsieur de Morgan, 'Excusez-moi, je prends une petite gorgée,' and sipped his wine. It was only then that I realised for Spassky the event was not a recreation of Reykjavik, 1972, but a day in the office, get it done, go home and forget about it.

I no longer knew what to say to him, so I thrust Fischer's book onto the table, open at Game 18, and asked him to sign it. When he realised what I'd given him, he chuckled and said, again to Monsieur de Morgan, 'Alors, c'était une bonne partie!' I'm not sure if he misunderstood my bad French, but for some reason he signed the book twice, once at the start of Game 18 and once on the title page, before he handed it back saying, 'Bon courage', then smiled at the Frenchman behind me in the queue.

I thanked him and moved to go before turning back and saying in English, 'Sorry Mr Spassky, I did have one question that I wanted to ask you.'

'Yes?'

'I've always wanted to know something. Can you please tell me why Fischer took that pawn on h2 in the first game of your match against him?'

He smiled at Monsieur de Morgan. 'Ah, this is what everyone wants to know, eh? Even now. After so many years.' Then Spassky looked directly at me for the first time and said, 'There is only one reason. Because he did not want draw. He wanted to win. He only wanted to win.' He took another sip of wine and said, 'By the way, there is very interesting move for you in our game – after I play Rc1 you have Nb4 ... it is complicated but maybe draw...' He announced about eight moves for both sides and said, 'And we get this ending with the opposite bishops... during the game I think draw.' He looked at the ceiling then added another ten moves or so, and said, 'But, maybe I can move my king. Alors, maybe win... but this is difficult.' He smiled at me like a rarely seen uncle who's shared his advice for what it's worth, then nodded at the guy behind me.

That night in medieval Dinard I got drunk for the first time in my life, taking advantage of France's legendary drinking age of sixteen. I found a small, almost empty bar with an old Eye of the Tiger pinball machine in the corner which I played between *je vourdraying demis*, excited by my entry into this adult world.

And I reflected on my encounter with Spassky. It was my first glimpse of a chess god and it had been terrible and awesome to see. Spassky had spent no more than a minute on any move he'd made at my position. He'd seen a move for me that I'd not even considered and analysed it cleanly, in a way that I'd have struggled to achieve with a chess set and a long afternoon, analysis that he'd effortlessly recalled a couple of hours later. He managed this while also beating the best players in Brittany. What would the guy be like one on one, with two hours on his clock? And this was Spassky past his prime, over a decade after his match with Fischer. What would he have been like in the sixties? However, rather than inspiring me to become like him, it made me realise my human limitations, my mortality and the impossibility of ever changing it. I'd previously had some intimations of this, such as when I finally understood Fischer's 11_NR5 against Byrne and doubted that I'd ever be able to build such a wonder. But I'd always rallied, always told myself that I just needed to study harder and play more, move closer to the abyss, and I'd be revealed to the world as the next Fischer. Spassky ended those illusions.

I left France on the deck of the ferry the following morning, sea spray bedabbled, breathing in the engine fumes and staring out at the horizon, nauseated with my life's first hangover. In my bag was my copy of *My 60 Memorable Games*, signed twice by Boris Spassky, and in my soul was the knowledge that I would never become world chess champion.

After that, I still spent time studying and playing chess but the all-consuming fire of Fischer had paled. I'd stopped at the edge of the abyss and taken a couple of steps back. Also, for the first time in my teenage life I had a competing interest – literature. Although, it was chess that led me there.

My new English A-Level teacher, Ms. Baker, aka the Bag Lady, suspecting that I wasn't reading anything, but knowing I was a chess player – I'd missed the first week of her lessons because of a tournament – offered me her own hardback copy of *The Luzhin Defense*. 'Why don't you try this one? It was written by a Russian but it's a good translation and you might like it; he's a terrific writer and I'm told that he knew a thing or two about chess.' I'd never heard of the book or the author and was immediately suspicious. The only good book about chess was by a grandmaster and contained moves, symbols and diagrams.

I started reading that Friday evening, apologising to my chess set waiting patiently for me on my desk. I finished it on Sunday evening with the set untouched. It was true – Nabokov understood chess and could describe its rich adventure, but there was something else, something unexpected. I was also transfixed by the power of his prose to light up the non-chess world. Never had I seen the world so clearly through someone else's eyes.

From *The Luzhin Defense* I moved on to his other books – amazed to find out that this Russian from Spassky's city of Leningrad also wrote in English. And what English it was. He could string words together like a series of exclamation mark chess moves. But his words were doing much more than chess moves – moves could only describe chess and, as beautiful as that could be, it remained a closed world. It took Nabokov to show me that literature was able to open up the world and celebrate all the beauty within it.

Nabokov became 'my writer' during that first year of the Sixth Form. I followed Humbert Humbert and his Dolly back and forth across the United States; I solved the giant chess puzzle of *Pale Fire;* and spent hours in the bath, my toe renewing the tap-warmth, with a huge mug of coffee and *Poems and Problems* – a combination of poetry and chess that was my *momentary vacuum into which rushed everything that I loved.*

In the second year, it was Joyce. When I read that Nabokov thought his writing was pat-ball compared to Joyce's championship game, I had to read this Irish guy. I wasn't sure about the tennis comparison, but if Nabokov was Alekhine – that sustained control of a puppet-master – then Joyce was Fischer – the all-encompassing brilliance. And *A Portrait of the Artist as a Young Man* shook up my consciousness as *My 60 Memorable Games* had done a few years earlier. Fischer's book had showed me what it was to be a chess player; Joyce's showed me what it was to be a writer, inspiring me with his love of language, search for knowledge, and monomaniac dedication to his art. Words and images were becoming more important to me than moves and combinations.

Then in *Ulysses* Joyce showed me what it is to be a human being. I went through it in that optimistic summer of Live Aid before going to university – the novel in front of me, Budgen's book of notes to my right, as in a previous summer I'd worked through Byrne and Nei's book on the Fischer-Spassky match, their analyses propped up next to the chessboard.

I'd return home at around three in the morning from my first job as a glass collector in a Dartford nightclub and sit in the kitchen – with its greasy ghost of my parents' evening meal – steadily drinking a four-pack of Carling, Pink Floyd on my Walkman, as I followed the great Leopold Bloom around Dublin, as he showed Stephen Dedalus how to move from his cold abstractions towards the warmth of humanity. I read until the sunlight gently woke the room and my dad would come downstairs to make a pot of his strong sweet tea – *You having one? Or you going up?* – before he left for work.

I sellotaped a postcard of Joyce on the wall above my desk, replacing the photo of Fischer at the Varna Olympiad. It was young Joyce standing in front of a greenhouse, wearing a baker boy hat, hands in pockets, head cocked arrogantly, staring out at the world into which he was about to go in search of the truth.

Reading Fischer made me want to play chess, reading Joyce made me want to write prose. It was sub-sub-Joycean tripe about life in Dartford – I didn't know anything about life in Dartford – but working on it was a good replacement for chess, trying to make words do what I wanted rather than the pieces, engaging with the materials of life rather than the sixty-four squares. There were a hundred decisions to make on the page rather than the chess board. How to develop the story, critical moments, successful endings. Calculation. Imagination. Creation. Losing myself in concentration, the element of time dropping out of my consciousness. And the same profound mining for the truth, mostly failing of course – uncovering the truth in fiction is even harder than in chess – but on those rare moments when you succeed the vision is so perfect that you want to cry out loud…

The England match is over. Nunn has stopped his clock. Nigel Short walks away. And I walk away, out of the Olympiad playing hall, back to the migrainey fug of my own tournament hall. And the wasteland of my position…

16

The Yugoslav is back in his chair, emitting a waft of freshly applied *eau de cigarette*, leaning back, seigneurially overseeing the board. I'm surprised he hasn't put a smoking jacket on. The pen is out of his mouth, he's stopped sweating, the worms have left his face, he's no longer interested in his clock. If he didn't know how good this was for him before, he does now.

I need to make a move here but what can I do? My bishop is hemmed in by my petrified pawns, my knight is lame, and my rook is running on square wheels. My most mobile piece is my king, but where's he going to go?

What have I done? How has it come to this? This is a disaster. I don't even want to look at the devastation in front of me. My position, so well made, so full of shiny potential, is in ruins, like a kid's favourite toy – his pristine model aeroplane – stamped on repeatedly by his father for a little understood misdemeanour. No spectators are marvelling at my board now – it's a sneer before moving on. They know.

The truth is that I'm lost here. I put my head in my hands, covering my eyes. I've got pins and needles in my head. Broken and scarred. I need an aspirin or three and a lie-down. A long period of oblivion. *There's no more pain now, son.*

How did this happen? Where did it all go wrong? Where did I chose the wrong turning? Where did I ruin it all?

It's hard to say, it's all so complicated. Was it my queen's marauding during his own queen's baroque retreat? No... there was no other way to continue the attack. My Tal-inspired bishop *and* knight sacrifice? No... if you remember, without that my attack was over. So... something earlier? I look down my grubby scoresheet, the record of my disgrace. No... all my moves after my rook sacrifice novelty were honest. So... the rook sacrifice itself, the 'brilliant novelty', the Patrick Moore Sacrifice? Hopelessly unsound? No, I needed to do that to buy time – without that, I'm joining Vykhovsky on the mortuary slab. So, where was the mistake? I must have made a mistake, you don't die without making a mistake. Even earlier? How far do I need to go back? I don't know, I just don't know – it's all too complicated. Maybe the whole Get-On-With-It Variation – 9... Nd7 – is moribund. Maybe Bobby was right after all and you have to play his blocking move on the queenside. Or maybe I shouldn't have played the King's Indian. Or got battered with Kolia last night. Or lost that stupid rook and bishop ending against Andic. Or blown all my money coming out to this Olympiad in Yugoslavia. Or taken up chess again instead of focussing on my research and writing. Or pushed Lauren away. Or given up on love...

But, how can you ever know what the right decision is? All you can do is look at the possibilities, assess the resulting positions, and plump for the one that looks best – the one that comes closest to the truth. You make your decision, but most of the time you have no idea what that truth is. 'Be true to yourself,' Polonius advised. But that's bullshit, of course. It's not enough to be true to yourself because what happens if your own truth is wrong? What happens if your truth is in fact an unsound combination? No, you need to be true to truth itself. But what is truth? Where is it? In chess it is that Perfect Form of a 5,000 ELO rating. But in life? I've no idea. Can someone please tell me?

I distanced myself from Lauren. I evaluated my position and thought that things would be better without her, assessing that I would increase my life prospects from slight advantage with her (*plus over equals*) to clear advantage without her (*plus over minus*). But was that the right decision?

Life, like chess, is one long regret.

I wish I could see her tonight after my game. I'd go to her student room and she'd be sitting cross-legged on her Indian rug, R.E.M. on her portable tape player, DMs peeking out from under her long witchy skirt, and I'd sit on her bed and laconically explain my loss, my failure, and she'd pout, 'Poor you', and look up at me with her big captivating smile, and I'd know that everything was going to be OK.

I remove my hands from my eyes and stare at the board again, although it's all meaningless, I've forgotten how to play – it looks like the game I watched between my dad and uncle when I was seven or eight and didn't know the rules. When I felt sorry for the bishops because they looked sad with their downturned mouths.

So, what am I going to do? In this game it's too late – I can't take any of my moves back… it's finished… but what about in life? What about with Lauren? And if I do, will it change anything?

WHOOOA! Hold on a minute! Hold on a cotton-picking

minute. My king is looking up trying to tell me something. He wants to be mobilised. Maybe there is a track for him, up the kingside... It's slow but maybe I can use my king to threaten the black's pawns over there. Buy some time to distract his stomping pieces. My king for a tempo. It's not as stupid as it looks. Maybe this is the cunning plan I need. Could I still save this with some nifty endgame play? Basic rule of the endgame – activate your king!

Why didn't I even consider this? I know all about activating your king in the endgame. This would be a great practical example for an endgame article in *Chess* – 'Renshaw uses his king aggressively in last-round save.'

But, I need to have a proper look at this. I take my head out of my hands and sit up, revived by the need to calculate, by having some work to do, some purpose. This is what I do...

But, even as I start to eke out some variations, I know that this is just fantasy, that the idea won't survive the reality of concrete moves, that there's nowhere for my king to go on the kingside, and that the poor bastard is losing his mind like Lear. Like me.

No, not this time, Baldrick. This one is over. There aren't going to be any magazine articles. 'Get real,' as the Americans say.

It's finished, collapsed like London Bridge. Not even one of Tal's incantations is going to put this one back together.

Why did this have to happen to me? Everything was going so well. And now as my bucket sinks into the well full of tears, so his raises up on high – or whatever that line is from *Richard II*. The Yugoslav was the one being crushed by an ocean of pressure, he was nearly hospitalised, and now look at him – relaxed, aware of his surroundings, identifying as a chess player.

And what about me? What am I identifying as? I'm not a chess player, that's for sure. Not like that Latvian over there on Board 1 with his proud quiff – clinical, unforgiving, Octavian – he's a real chess player. Only eighteen or nineteen, a protégé of Tal, he's already defeated grandmasters and will surely be one soon. What have I done? What have I achieved? I couldn't get through the British Championships without crying myself to sleep because the big boys were beating me up. I was a non-entity at the Lloyds Bank Masters. I can't even beat a washed-up Yugoslav master. No, I'm not a chess player... nor was meant to be.

What am I then? A fool? What am I doing with my life? I've lost Lauren, I haven't written a word of my PHD, haven't written *anything* for months, I haven't read anything apart from chess books. I haven't seen my poor mum in weeks. And all for what? Pushing myself towards the abyss because I think that I'll find the Holy Grail of chess in there? And I don't even know what that Grail is, what it is that I'm searching for. I'm never going to be world champion or a grandmaster, or even a master. It makes no sense. Why can't I be like those old boys at Dartford Chess Club who used to infuriate me in my Fischer-tinged youth. They would enjoy their game on Thursday night and then forget about chess for a week while they returned to their nine-to-five lives – chatting with the missus, weeding the garden, snooker on the TV. Like my father.

I look at the high windows, but there are no answers up there, only an endless darkening sky, out of which soft snow flakes are swirling against the panes.

But that's just it. I use chess to escape from 'normal life'. I know, even as I peer into the chess abyss, that the Grail is not in there, that the Grail doesn't exist. But I carry on with the journey because while I'm on it I don't have to think about other things. About life. That's what I was doing as a teenager, because I didn't want to deal with school, friends, warring parents, becoming an adult. My hero was someone who had also rejected life. At university, I managed to pull away from all that, and finally found someone who understood me, who accepted me, who loved my weirdness, and who helped me embrace life. But it was too much – afraid of getting caught up in the thorny brambles of life, I fell back to the straight clean paths of chess. But they don't lead anywhere. They're an illusion. Chess can be a sublimely beautiful art – but it's not a substitute for life. Spassky realised that, Fischer didn't. Chess will always be cold and sterile. There is no human warmth on the chess board. There is no love.

I know all this, of course, but sometimes I just don't apply it. It's like the sickening King's Indian endgame. I have the knowledge but not the wisdom to avoid it.

Chess is not beautiful enough to waste your life on.

After this tournament, it's time to return to life. I'm going to start working on my PHD again, exchange chess theory for literary theory. Start writing again, put good prose into my notebooks rather than bad chess moves. Go to pubs to talk to people instead of playing pinball. Go and see my mum in Dartford. Get in contact with Lauren again. Speak to Lauren again.

I want to tell someone all this. I feel like grabbing my opponent by his seventies shirt collar. 'Well played my friend, good game... look, instead of a post-mortem on the game could we do a post-mortem on my life instead?'

A grand sigh wheezes out from one of the players down the boards to my right. The frustrated death rattle of another defeated chess player.

The mellow afternoon sunlight was seeping in through the high windows of the University Main Library, glazing the long table where I was starting the research for my PHD. Bent over my battered edition of *Ulysses* (my eighteenth birthday present – *Are you sure that's what you want, son?*), safe in the churchy smell of the old books, head in hands, I was trying to follow Stephen Dedalus' calculations that prove Hamlet's grandson is Shakespeare's grandson, and that he himself is the ghost of his own father…

A blubbery sigh disturbed me from my analysis.

I looked up, adjusting to the air after surfacing from my deep dive of concentration. There was no one in the seat opposite me – only young cocky Stephen Dedalus, leaning forward on his ashplant stick, looking at me coldly. Diagonally opposite to my right, a knight's move away, was a student who looked like Plain Jane from *Neighbours*. Same lean mouth, small nose, blonde fringe. Although she was skinnier and flat chested. In a flouncy dress, and wearing large framed glasses. She had a copy of *Coriolanus* propped up in a splash of sunlight, black Bic in her mouth, frowning at the text. I looked up at the high windows and could just see the glinting edge of the Telecom Tower's silvery coronet. She took the pen out of her mouth and blew up into her fringe.

'That bad, eh?' I punted as an opening gambit, my confidence boosted by the Shakespeare connection and the little-girl frustration.

She blinked, took the pen out of her mouth, and slowly looked up from her book and across at me. 'I'm sorry?' Tight thin mouth.

'Erm, I mean it's quite tricky, isn't it?'

'What is?' Posh accent rather than Australian.

'Erm, that play, *Coriolanus*.'

'Yes, I suppose it is – some of the words are anyway.'

'Yes, exactly, that's exactly what I mean... some of the vocabulary he uses. Maybe I can help you? I actually know that play quite well.' I held my *Ulysses* aloft for her to see, as if that provided evidence for my knowledge of *Coriolanus*.

She stared at me through those big wire-rimmed glasses, as if we were playing a blitz game and she suspected, she knew, that all my moves were lies.

'Okaaaay... well, I'm not sure.... Do you know precisely what 'verkrueppelt' means?'

"Verkrueppelt'? Which character says that?'

'Coriolanus.'

'Mmm, does he? Not sure to be honest... although it sounds Anglo-Saxon to me – you know Shakespeare liked to mix in Old English words to supplement, to enhance, his wide Latin vocabulary?'

'No, I don't think I knew that but...'

'Yes, yes, if you think of his 'unparalleled lass' that he uses to describe Cleopatra, for example – that's a striking juxtaposition of Anglo-Saxon and Latinate words to demonstrate both sides of Cleopatra, the earthy and the sophisticated – and then also in Macbeth we find ...'

'Ah yes, that does seem to be a *striking juxtaposition* – but 'verkrueppelt', it's actually not Anglo-Saxon, it's German.'

'German?'

'Yes, this isn't Shakespeare's *Coriolanus* that I'm reading, but Bertolt Brecht's *Coriolanus*. Or *Coriolan*.' She held her book up high to show me the name of its author and its correct title. 'In German. I'm trying to read it for my master's thesis.'

'Ah yes, of course. Brecht's *Coriolanus*. *Coriolan*. Sorry, I can't really help you on that one, I'm afraid – I don't know any German.' Apart from *Luft*, *Zwischenzug* and *Zugzwang*. 'I know a bit of French, but I guess that's not going to help, is it?'

'No, I don't think it would.'

All my pawns had gone and it was time to return to Stephen Dedalus. Then she smiled at me for the first time – the thin mouth wondrously transformed into perfect teeth, thickened lips, the top one slightly turned upwards, highlighted by shining dimples – and said, 'Anyway, it doesn't matter, I can work out what it means. But, I'm sorry, what was that you were you going to say about Macbeth? I'd like to hear more of your *striking juxtapositions*.' She gave a wry half-smile.

'Hey, you're making fun of me.'

She shook her head, blonde fringe swaying above the steel of her glasses. 'No, not at all.'

'Look, I'll let you get back to your play and I'll...'

'No, sorry. Seriously, I'm really interested in that sort of thing. I love words and language and things. And I'd love you to explain it to me. Really. Look, sorry, I think I need a break from this stuff... and I'm addicted to the carrot cake they do in the café... and you look like maybe you could do with a break...'

I wonder what she's doing now? Would she still want to be my *future tense*? Or is it too late? Crazy Kolia would tell me that it's never too late. *To hell with everything else, man. Speak to her. Better than that – go and find her. Tell her how you feel, tell her that you make mistake. Show her how much you want her – go through the wall, man.*

Is that what I should do? Call Kolia and tell him that I'm going with him to Berlin… go and find Lauren.

My heart is pumping at the thought. And when I first see her, sitting at the table of a Berlin beer hall, she'll look up at me gravely and shake her head. Then she'll give me her big well-hello-it's-Sammy smile. And it'll be OK.

That's it, I'm going to call Kolia, from the phone box down the street outside the Sports Hall.

But I need to make a move first. But what to play? I don't really have a move here. A pawn up and I'm nearly in *zugzwang*. *Zugzwang* – that horrible onomatopoeia for contorted agony where the slightest flinch only increases the pain. Any move is just a red flag to his hooded hordes swarming over my position. I feel like Saemisch who was a piece up against Nimzowitsch and couldn't move a thing – the 'Immortal Zugzwang'. 1923. I say that, but how did Saemisch feel? We don't know. We hear the triumphalism of Nimzowitsch but not the voice of the defeated Saemisch. Did he have that headachy sense of loss? Did he feel sick as he stared at the horrible reality of his position – lost with White in just over twenty moves? Crushed like a cockroach under Nimzovitch's big boot. Did he question his sense of himself as a chess player? Start re-evaluating his personal life? Friedrich Saemisch – who was he? I don't know anything about him. He's just a name. A victim in the games collections of great players. Although he gave his name to one of the most feared lines against the King's Indian – one that even Fischer didn't like to face. And didn't he beat Capablanca at some point or am I imagining that? I'll have to check that when I get home. No, I won't check that. I'm going to Berlin. It doesn't matter who Saemisch was or what he did. I'm going to be staying away from the chess books, giving them away, burning them like they did to poor Don Quixote's library to protect him from any further madcap, futile, self-destructive adventures…

But I need to play something. I can't just sit here thinking about Don Quixote as my clock runs down. The clock face that now looks away from me in contempt.

I could move my knight – no, that's nonsense. I could move my rook – no, that's nonsense. I can't move my bishop. I could move my king – but he's got nowhere to go. All pawn moves create more weaknesses. I can't move a thing…

I think it's time to call it a day.

Normally the thought of resigning freezes my heart with dread. Something you just don't want to think about. Like contemplating suicide.

But it's OK. I've accepted it.

I've failed but I was here. On this Monday morning in Novi Sad, with the rest of them – the German kid, Andic, Animal, Pavlovic. My opponent. We were here, we did it. And I'm already feeling a weird kind of nostalgia.

But now it's time to move on. It's time to put my lands in order. Time to move out of chess time and back into the world. Into real life. I flex the muscles off my right hand like a starfish. Here we go…

I extend my hand to my opponent. He looks up at me, meets my eyes head on for the first time, and takes my hand like I'm pulling him out of the sea. 'Well played,' I croak.

He lets out a prolonged sigh and shakes his head. 'No, no, no, is you play well. I am lucky. Very lucky. I am dead. I almost resign. Zen I see zis queen move.' He charts out his queen's odyssey with his tobacco-stained forefinger.

'Yeh, I didn't see it. It was a very good idea.'

'Only idea. Only idea. Without zis I am dead. But you have attack. Still. Strong attack. You take all pieces back wiz queen but you can move rook. Wiz strong attack.'

'OK, I missed that one.' OK, maybe I did have other possibilities, other chances. Roads not taken. But it doesn't matter now.

'But you play brilliant. Zis rook sacrifice,' he points at a8. 'Zis bishop and knight sacrifice,' he points at h3. 'Brilliant.' He shakes his head. 'Brilliant.'

'And did you see the possible queen sacrifice variation,' I whisper.

'Yes, yes, of course, so beautiful.' He shakes his head again and looks at the board in contemplation. 'Sooooo beautiful. Zis why we play chess, yes?'

I sign my scoresheet and hand it to him, disturbing his reverie.

'Yes, yes, sank you,' he whispers, and scrawls his own sheet before passing it over for me to sign – '1-0. F. Mitrovic.' 'We must do analizes of game. Together. Is soooo much for us to see, yes? We go to analizes room?'

'Yes, I would love to but, sorry, I have something I must do first. Maybe in fifteen minutes, OK? I find you?'

'Of course, of course. I look at games. Very good. I wait you.' He wraps himself in his sleety grey cardigan/coat and stands up. I also stand up.

Mitrovic. Looking up at me, random tufts of hair sticking up on his head, pressing his plastic bag of chess magazines/bulletins to his chest with both arms, like a child with his teddy bear before going to bed.

I smile at him as I put my jacket back on. He smiles back.

No, you are not the enemy, or a Yugoslav, or a Serb, or a Croat, but a chess player. My partner. *Mon semblable. Mon frère.*

The old arbiter in his long coat is running over the fields.

I put my Parker in the inside pocket of my jacket and feel the squidgy rubber rook of Lauren's keyring and the rough cardboard surface of the cigarette packet with Kolia's number. I pick up the opened Mars Bar, suddenly hungry. I'm about to go – out of the playing hall, down the corridor, out of the Sports Hall entrance, down the steps, out into the peaceful snow – when I notice that chess time is still running. I lean over and stop my clock.

THE END

ACKNOWLEDGEMENTS

I would like to thank Alison Williams and Claire Wingfield for their meticulous readings of early drafts and their wise suggestions.

A big thank you to Stephen Romer for the use of his fantastic writer's retreat in the Loire Valley.

Thanks to Elisabeth for coming to Margate with me and for everything else.

Thanks to Jon for his comments during our late-night analysis sessions.

Many thanks too to James Essinger and Charlotte Mouncey of The Conrad Press.

And thanks to chess players past and present, especially those whom I have played against, talked with, or admired from afar – I salute you all.